baby blue

MICHELLE D. KWASNEY

baby
blue

Henry Holt and Company

New York

I am grateful to Captain Michael B. Wall and Sergeant Dorothy Gagne of the Northampton Police Department, Mary Kociela of the Northwestern District Attorney's office, the reference librarians at Forbes Library, David at Dynamite Records, and countless others who patiently answered e-mail and phone questions during the writing of this novel.

Special thanks to my Tuesday night critique group, the Hatfield, Massachusetts, chapter of the Society of Children's Book Writers and Illustrators, and my editor and mentor, Christy Ottaviano, who saw in those early seedlings what *Baby Blue* might become and skillfully guided its growth.

Henry Holt and Company, LLC
Publishers since 1866
115 West 18th Street
New York, New York 10011
www.henryholt.com

Henry Holt is a registered trademark of Henry Holt and Company, LLC
Copyright © 2004 by Michelle D. Kwasney
All rights reserved.
Distributed in Canada by H. B. Fenn and Company Ltd.

Library of Congress Cataloging-in-Publication Data
Kwasney, Michelle D.
Baby Blue / Michelle D. Kwasney.
p.   cm.
Summary: In western Massachusetts in 1976, still grieving and guilt-ridden over her father's drowning, twelve-year-old Blue is dealt another blow when her older sister, Star, runs away to escape their stepfather's violence against their mother.
[1. Wife abuse—Fiction. 2. Family problems—Fiction. 3. Stepfathers—Fiction. 4. Sisters—Fiction. 5. Massachusetts—History—20th century—Fiction.] I. Title.
PZ7.K9757Ba 2004   [Fic]—dc22   2003056579

ISBN 0-8050-7050-8
First edition–2004
Printed in the United States of America on acid-free paper. ∞

10 9 8 7 6 5 4 3 2 1

To Barbara,
who listened first,
for never not believing

baby blue

prologue

I dreamt about Pa again. Our *real* Pa.

He was at the bottom of the river. His face was swollen, round and white like the moon. He stretched his hand out to show me something. Something shiny. Something small. I couldn't see what it was.

Pa had on his lucky shirt in the dream, the blue and white one he'd wear when he'd sneak off in the middle of the night and drive to Canandaigua to play the horses. Drive all night from western Massachusetts to the far side of New York State—an awfully wide state at that—so he'd be there in the morning when the track opened.

Mama and my big sister, Star, and me'd never hear him leave. We'd find his note on the kitchen table come morning. It always said the same thing: *Took a drive to New York to clean out my thoughts.* But Pa's thoughts weren't all that got cleaned out on those trips. The red clay pot on the shelf over the sink I'd made Mama in art class—the one she kept her waitressing tips in—that always got cleaned out, too.

Pa wore his lucky shirt to Canandaigua and back a hundred times, but it only worked for him once. I'll remember *that* night forever. Mama and Star and me had waited supper lots later than usual. The hamburgers sat in the fry pan, shriveled up to nothing. Mama's tossed salad had wilted. Finally, Mama and me ate. Not Star, though. She waited for Pa.

Pa showed up close to ten, his arms weighed down with fancy shopping bags from the stores downtown. Star was in the middle of painting her nails when he appeared at the door. She leapt at him and hugged him hard, smearing Shade #41, Warm Strawberry Glaze, all across the back of his lucky shirt.

I was behind, waiting to hug him next.

Pa stooped over. "Hey, Blue. What's my baby up to?"

I wrapped my arms around his neck. His coat smelled like hay. His face was cool from the night air. "Missing you," I whispered in his ear.

Mama looked up from the S&H Green Stamps she'd been pasting in her book. I waited to see if she was done being mad, if she would hug him, too. But there was no time to think. Pa tossed an envelope bursting with twenty-dollar bills on the table in front of her.

Mama looked stunned as a game show winner. She counted the money out loud. "Jeez, Louise, Roy. There's over three thousand dollars in here!"

Pa was beaming. He lifted Mama off her chair, wrapping his tanned arms around her skinny waist. "See, Cecilia, honey, I told you I'd win big someday!"

Star eyed the shopping bags while Mama ran her thumb back and forth across the crisp row of new bills. I felt sick with what I was thinking, how—sure as tears come dicing an onion—Pa would take off again. Maybe that very same night even. And the envelope overflowing with big green bills wouldn't be all he'd take with him. Everybody's private dream of what three thousand dollars might buy would follow him out that door, too: The flower shop Mama'd fantasized about; the art lessons Pa'd been promising me since third grade; Star's new clarinet, so she wouldn't have to go on renting that old one half the school'd slobbered on.

I looked around me. It was obvious I was the only one having such depressing thoughts.

Star dove into her bag, plowing through the crisp tissue paper poofing out the top. "Oh, Pa! I love you!" she yelled, holding up the size-ten Frye boots she'd taken to worshipping in a store window downtown. Their toes gleamed like fresh tar in the dim kitchen light. She slipped them on and whirled around, her gauze skirt brushing the tops of them.

Pa sat down next to Mama. They held hands.

Another whirl around. Star was just like her name; she lit up anything that didn't already sparkle. She kissed Pa's bald spot, then grabbed my arm. "Dance with me, Blue!"

"No!" I said, clutching the seat of my chair. But a lot of good that did. It was true what Pa said—Star could coax the candy shell off an M&M. One good yank and I was upright, holding tight to Star's shoulders to keep from toppling over.

Pa reached behind him to click on the transistor radio. It was set on his favorite AM station, the same one I won a six-pack of cola at for being the seventeenth caller. "Hey!" Pa hollered. "My favorite song!"

"Mine, too!" Star yelled, reaching for the dial. The music shot high as a firecracker on the Fourth of July, the kitchen exploding with color and light and sound.

Star spun us in wide, dizzy circles, her long red hair swishing side to side. Faster.

I felt woozy, heavy with heat. My eyes tried to land somewhere. On the dish drainer. On the stove light. The crooked window blind. But they flew by too fast.

"Take it to the limit . . . ," Pa sang.

Faster, faster, Star spun us.

Dish drainer, stove light, window blind . . .

Star threw her head back, her smile lighting my path.

I couldn't fight it. My mouth fell open. A laugh escaped. I threw my head back too.

It was me who made Pa promise to take us to the river the next day. It was my way of keeping him close to home, of seeing to it the three thousand dollars stayed put.

The current was strong that afternoon. Pa and Star trudged toward Big Rock with their fishing poles. Star's the squeamish type, one of those people who gets all upset if they step on an anthill by accident, so I never could see her taking a liking to something mildly barbaric like piercing some poor fish in the face with a sharp hook. I figured it was the time with Pa she liked.

"Be careful!" Mama hollered. "*Both* of you!" I knew she meant Pa. Star was on the swim team at school, but Pa—well, as Mama once put it—Pa'd need a lifejacket to take a bubble bath.

Upriver, two young boys sat on a knoll skipping stones. Other than them, it was just the four of us.

Mama and me picked wild raspberries in the thick brush nearby. I was eating most of what I picked. Every now and then, I'd glance back at the river, at Pa pulling on a fish he'd caught. Star was laughing at how funny he looked with his feet spread wide on the slimy stone, trying to keep his balance while the fish took *him* for a ride. Their echoes ricocheted off the rocky hills while Mama's berries made little thunking noises in the metal pan.

I was feeling good, through and through. That kind of good that bears down on your heart so fiercely you don't know whether to laugh or cry.

Then I heard the scream.

Mama and me threw our berry pans and ran. The stainless steel clanged on the stone. Bells. That's what they sounded like. Bells calling for help. We stood at the edge, gasping as Star's and Pa's fishing poles bobbed past. Mama cupped her hands over her mouth. *"Star! Roy!"* she hollered. The hills threw the words back. "Where *are* you? What's wrong?"

Star popped out of the water, wiping the wet from her eyes. She pointed upriver, to where the two boys had decided to go in. "The little one," she yelled. "He couldn't swim!" The current pushed at the fringe of her cut-offs. She stepped back, steadying herself. "We're trying to save him."

"We?" The wind had picked up. Mama pushed the hair out of her eyes. "No! Not your pa! He can't—"

Star was shivering. "He wouldn't listen to me!"

"Look!" I yelled.

Pa's head shot up, his red hair like a splash of fire on the murky gray-green water.

"Oh, God!" Star screamed. "Pa, I'm right here!"

But Pa's head disappeared again, just as the little boy's rose up. The older kid called out his name. Jay-something. Jay-something held up his hand. The older kid swam toward it.

Water hammered the shore. The older kid pulled Jay-something in, sitting him beside Mama's feet while he coughed and sputtered and blew shiny bubbles out his nose.

"Pa!" Star yelled. "Pa, where'd you go?" She dove below the surface.

I counted while I watched for her. Nine. Ten. Eleven. Twelve. Star sprang up. Gulped air. Ducked under a second time. A third.

Still no Pa.

Mama laid a towel across Jay-something's shoulders and started in. I tried to follow her. "No!" she snapped. "Wait here. Keep an eye on the boy."

I could've cared less about the boy.

Mama's legs moved slow against the current. "Roy!" she called. "Rooooooy!" She was in up to her waist, her body wavering like she'd been drinking. "Roy, please! Can you hear me, Roy?" She waded in deeper.

"Go back!" Star shouted. "Go back, Mama. It's dangerous!"

I tasted the raspberries coming up in my throat. My body lunged forward. I grabbed my stomach, throwing up in the tall grass. Seeds peppered my sour tongue. I wiped my chin on the shoulder of my T-shirt.

The brush by the wild raspberries rustled. I heard a voice behind me.

"Over there, look!" a man yelled. Then a second one. "Let's go!"

I watched them dart across the river stones. The shorter one kicked a berry pan. Its tinny echo slammed the hills.

"Hurry!" I yelled. "It's our pa. He can't swim so good!"

The men stripped down to their boxer shorts and ran in. The shorter one swam out to Mama. The tall skinny one rushed to Star, laying his hand on her shoulder. She started toward me, an eerie look in her eyes I'd never seen before. I reached for Pa's summer jacket, laying it across her shoulders. It smelled like him, even without him in it.

The shorter man looped his arm through Mama's, guiding her in as she walked backward, stumbling, calling to the dark, choppy water. "Roy? Roy, honey, please answer me!"

The men searched for Pa. The sun perched on the purple hills. The river turned black.

I pulled Star's dripping hair away from her neck. "You're shaking," I said, closing Pa's jacket over the front of her.

Her lips were a funny shade of blue. "Where's Pa?" Star whispered. "Where is he?"

part one

one

The air conditioner was broken in Beau Silver's Silver-spoon Diner. Even the red YOU ARE HERE dot on the Massachusetts map by the front door was sweating.

I followed Jinx to the old part, near the grill. The air was sticky, thick with the smell of bacon grease and sweat. The red, white, and blue crepe-paper streamers Beau'd hung for the Bicentennial Parade rippled below the ceiling fans.

Jinx picked a booth beside the jukebox. He dropped a quarter in the slot, and we sat down, him on one side, me on the other. I kept seeing that red YOU ARE HERE dot. Like the light that stays after a camera flash pops.

The grill hissed behind me. "Order up!" Beau Silver yelled.

Mama zipped past, four Tuesday specials balanced down the length of her arm. You would never catch me attempting such a feat! I was the klutz who always managed to kick over the orange cones during relay races on field day. "Ours are up next," she said, flashing us a smile.

I smiled back. Jinx didn't bother. He hummed along to the jukebox, staring at the rig parked outside the window. A rig like Pa used to drive.

Mama returned with our plates.

It was Tuesday, Meat Loaf Night. All you can eat for $1.79. Jinx ordered fries, so just to be different, I asked for mashed potatoes. Mama had her usual: a tossed salad with blue-cheese dressing and a Pepsi Light. Mama didn't eat meat. She claimed it was on account of my being born in the meat department of Frank's Hometown Market. There she was, smack-dab in the middle of ordering a pound of cube steak when she went into labor. Frank himself brought me into the world, kicking and sliding on the cold gray tile in the back room, a leg of lamb swaying on a hook over our heads. That's the story I was told, anyway.

Mama undid her apron but left the HI! I'M CECILIA! pin on her uniform. She slid in beside me, her heavy pockets drooping to the sides like ears on a puppy dog. A lump of change pressed against my hip. "You're early," she said.

Jinx shot Mama a lopsided grin. "Afternoon foreman shut us down." He tapped a cigarette on the table and lit it, blowing smoke rings that floated straight up and didn't dissolve till the ceiling fan got ahold of them. "Moron's got wood chips for brains. I'll be glad when I'm on nights again, away from his sorry . . ." His eyes wandered back outside.

I felt a string on the hem of the shorts I'd made in Home Ec. I pulled and pulled till it snapped loose. "So, Mama," I said, "was it busy today?"

I stared at Mama staring at Jinx staring at whatever he was staring at. I got a good look at her face. I was on the side with the eye that got hit. Mama'd gobbed skin-colored cream on the bruise, then powder over that, but the bump still showed.

Mama rubbed her neck. "That it was, Blue. That it was."

A man who looked something like our real pa hopped in the rig parked by the window. I watched him start it up. Its rhythm rumbled, deep in my ribs. The truck pulled out, slapping a square of sun on our table.

I dug a green bean loose from the sticky mashed-potato lump. I worked my food into three separate piles and stared at the center of the plate where nothing touched anymore.

I felt Mama watching. "Anybody hungry?"

I didn't get to answer. Jinx did. "Now that you mention it, Ceil, I'm really not all that hungry. But I sure am *thirsty* as the devil." He signaled Beau Silver, pointing toward the middle handle on the beer tap.

"Lyle," Mama said—Lyle is Jinx's real name—"I thought you were working on your truck tonight." His old Ford pickup needed a muffler bad.

Jinx snuffed out his cigarette in the silver spoon-shaped ashtray and gulped down half the mug of beer Beau brought him. The frost melted where his fingers had been. "Don't start on me, Ceil."

Mama looked away. She poured dressing on her salad, sliding the lettuce and tomato and cucumber round and round in the fake wood bowl.

I took a bite of my meat loaf.

Jinx sucked down the rest of his beer, then waved to Beau Silver for another. Beau wiped his hands on his greasy apron and the mug disappeared.

I kept wishing Star'd walk in. It didn't seem to matter that she'd been gone a month almost. 'Cause every time the door swung open, I watched for her, hair wet from swim practice, smelling of chlorine, sunglasses resting low on her nose.

Beau brought Jinx a second beer. This time the glass wasn't frosty. The top didn't have any foam. The beer looked like pee. I pictured Star and me in the girls' bathroom on the other end of the diner, hooting at the thought of Jinx gulping down somebody's pee. Beau Silver's pee, maybe.

Jinx raised the mug. The bump in his throat bobbed up and down while he swallowed. Four big gulps.

Mama plunged her fork through a thick pile of lettuce. "How was your class party?" she asked me. We'd had our end-of-the-year picnic at Riverside Park that day.

"It was fun," I answered. "Bonnie Price and me went on the roller coaster nine times. Eddie Cumberland threw up on the Scrambler."

Mama smiled. "Sounds exciting. Was five dollars enough?"

"Plenty. I even had money left for games. Bonnie and me won matching mood rings." I flashed the stone at her. Pure black.

"Hey, Blue"—Jinx stuck a giant wedge of meat loaf in his mouth, talking and chewing at the same time— "seventh grade's been quite a drain on the old economy, hasn't it?"

My stomach grabbed hard on the meat loaf. "What do you mean?"

He stuck a handful of French fries in his mouth, smashing them into a pocket on the side of his face. "Well, seems you just needed five bucks a few weeks ago for some book fair"—the lump in his cheek bounced to the other side—"and five more, right after, for some dumb present—"

"It *wasn't* dumb," I said. My voice was calm but tight.

Mama's hand was on my knee under the table. I knew the squeeze meant stop, but I didn't.

"It was for our English teacher, Mrs. Fitzhugh. She's retiring." A truck pulled in where the other one had been. A huge, cool shadow fell over Mama and me. "We got her an engraved watch. All of us did—I mean, we all chipped in."

Jinx's fork slammed the table. "Don't you mean your *parents* all chipped in?"

The people in the next booth turned to look.

Mama squeezed my knee again. Harder. See, she hadn't learned yet what Star and me figured out a long time ago—if Jinx was looking to start a fire, he'd start a fire. And he'd find kindling anywhere he could.

Mama reached to touch Jinx's arm. He pulled it back so hard the seat on his side reared up then fell forward.

The people in the next booth got up to leave.

"Lyle," Mama whispered. "Let's not argue here. Please. I've got to work with these people."

Jinx glared at her.

I heard the grill hiss behind me. I heard Beau Silver yell "Order up!" Then I felt the sudden cold splash of

Mama's Pepsi Light as Jinx leapt up and the table tipped toward us.

Beau Silver darted through the small swinging door at the end of the counter.

Jinx tore down the aisle.

Mama's eyes got red. Then wet. Her cakey makeup started to run, and her bruise—a secret she thought she'd buried—floated into view.

Beau lifted the table off our legs. He used his rag to dab a blob of blue cheese off Mama's shoulder. Ketchup was smeared on her chest.

I watched out the window as Jinx jumped into his rusty black pickup, gunning the gas pedal hard. A cloud of thick, smelly smoke clung close on all sides.

Mama avoided the eyes staring her down. "Come on, Blue," she said. "Let's go wash up in the little girls' room."

Jinx's truck coughed exhaust as it roared across the parking lot.

I brushed his French fries off the vinyl seat and slid out, relishing the loud clanging noise his muffler made dropping loose in a giant pothole.

two

The tail of the mermaid tattoo on Beau's arm scrunched up and stretched out while he mopped around our booth. I could hear his breath each time the mermaid stretched. A hard, scratchy breath like two fall leaves getting scraped together.

"You two go on home," he said. "I'll look after the rest."

Mama used her tip money to pay for dinner and however many mugs of beer Jinx had guzzled down. We counted what was left out front. "Forty-five cents in nickels," Mama said. "It's not even enough for the darn bus." That's about as close to cursing as Mama gets.

A man in a pale blue leisure suit squeezed in beside us, dropping change in the newspaper box. Mama didn't notice him staring. "Beau'll loan us the money," she said. "I'll just go back in and ask him for—"

I grabbed her arm. "Mama, don't!" The man looked

straight at me. Our eyes locked. He flashed me a phony smile. I stared him down till he looked away. My voice came out gritty. "We'll *walk*."

Mama licked a finger and rubbed dried ketchup off my neck. "Oh, Blue, be serious. It's over five miles and hot as all get out."

I didn't fuss about the spit thing, like usual. And I didn't give her that look she doesn't care for, either. I just started to walk, and her hand fell away.

I turned when I got to the edge of the parking lot. "You coming along, Mama?"

"Jeez, Louise!" she grumbled, stomping to catch up to me.

꧁

The river was the halfway point.

Our heads were sweating in the late-day sun. I had blisters on both my heels. Mama'd started smelling like blue cheese gone bad.

I looked out at the water. The light danced across Big Rock.

Jinx is at it again, Pa. I try to look after Mama, just like I promised you, but it's getting harder all the ti— The water rushed sideways. It felt like the bridge was moving. I stumbled.

Mama stepped closer, catching my elbow. "You all right, Blue?"

I closed one eye so I couldn't see the water. "I'm fine," I said. A big, fat lie.

We came to the end of the bridge. A truck thundered by that looked like Jinx's, except without all the rust. "Hey, Mama," I asked, "you want to play the license plate game?" It was something Star'd made up.

I could tell she wasn't crazy about the idea. "Sure," she said anyway. "Go ahead, you pick first."

I searched for an out-of-state plate. (Massachusetts plates were skimpy, they only had one letter.) A tan station wagon from New York drove past. I called out the letters.

"E . . . G . . . P . . . ," Mama repeated, thinking.

"I know!" I tugged on her sleeve. "Eating Grape Popsicles makes your tongue turn purple."

"Fast, Miss Smarty Pants."

I smiled. I liked being called smart. Pa used to tease me when I'd bring home straight As. He'd sing, "Smarty, Smarty, had a party, and nobody showed up," but I knew he was proud.

I picked again, on account of being first. "BDN."

Mama's head shot up. "I've got one! Billy's Diapers Need changing *bad.*"

It was obvious Mama'd forgotten Star's rule about not using proper names, but she was looking so pleased I let it go. "Okay," I said. "Your turn."

We stopped at the light by the crosswalk. Mama looked the cars over good. "OST," she announced.

The light turned. We crossed. The shade from a tree cooled my shoulders. "Here goes," I said, cutting up. "Our Scummy Toilet needs cleaning."

Mama's lip curled. "Ewwww, gross."

I started laughing.

Mama did, too. Her eyes teared and she doubled forward. "Oh, Blue, stop! I—I've got to pee! Where's that—" She tried to stand upright. "Where's that scummy toilet?" She looked around, playing serious, like she might just find it in the street.

We laughed on and off the rest of the way back. I kept stealing glances at Mama's face. At how her eyes crinkled at the corners when she laughed, how her cheeks balled up, round and red like polished apples. I couldn't help thinking—even with her hair flattened down with sweat and her bruise shining like a full blue moon—she looked awful pretty.

Mama pushed a strand of hair behind my ear and rested her hand on my shoulder, picking at that ketchup blob again.

I didn't pull away this time. And not just 'cause Mama wasn't wielding one of those spit-on fingers, either. I didn't pull away 'cause Mama was being plain old Mama. And I'd missed her something fierce.

$\underset{\sim}{\text{\Large \&}}$

The next morning, I woke to the whistle of Mama's teakettle, a sound that put a smile on my face. If Jinx were home, the percolator would be popping. He claimed Mama's instant coffee made hamster piss look good.

Mama was sitting at the kitchen table, rubbing muscle balm on her shoulders. The water in the vase of flowers Jinx had given her that past week was starting to smell.

I bent to kiss her cheek. It was hot from a sunburn, like mine. I poured some apple juice, then slid my chair close. "Here," I said, reaching for the tube, squeezing it into my palm. "I'll do your neck."

Mama's head rocked forward. "Lyle didn't come home last night."

My fingers tingled as I rubbed. "I noticed."

"Your Pa did that once or twice," Mama said. "Darn gambling bug."

I hated when Mama compared Pa to Lyle. "Want to sit outside?" I asked. My thighs made a ripping noise on the vinyl cushion as I stood up.

"Why not? Can't be any muggier out there."

Mama followed me into the shade. The overgrown bushes pushed against Jinx's rusty metal shed. Through the mesh of the chain-link fence I could see two teenage boys walking the railroad tracks, passing a brown-bag bottle back and forth. I sat on the damp grass. Mama squatted on the stump of the dead dogwood, the one Jinx's landlord cut down after the ice storm last winter. I missed that tree; it was the only thing that flowered in that barren, bristly backyard.

In our old yard, behind the house we had with Pa, we had loads of flowers. Stock and hollyhocks and larkspur Mama'd started from seed. Lilac bushes so full they spilled across my bedroom window like purple curtains. I would wake mornings to their honeyed scent, the dull hum of bees on their plump blossoms.

Mama *tried* planting in Jinx's backyard. After we moved in he brought her potted flowers nearly every day. She'd dig holes in the dry, sandy soil, coaxing it along with peat moss and manure. But every last one of those pretty plants shriveled up and died.

"Whatcha thinking?" Mama asked.

"I was wondering why we had to move here. Why we couldn't have stayed in our old house."

"Blue, honey, we've been through this. Lyle didn't want us starting our life together in another man's shadow.

Besides"—Mama picked the straggly clover sprouting around the dead trunk—"I like the house Lyle rents."

"You do?" I studied the green crust growing under the roof shingles. "What's so great about it?"

"Well, for one thing, the house we had with your pa didn't have a cellar. A family needs storage space." Mama rolled the clover stems back and forth. "And we had to drive forever to get to a store. Those back roads were terrible in the winter. This is lots more convenient. Downtown's close. The highway's close. The bus goes right by."

"Mama, you wouldn't need the bus if Lyle hadn't made you sell the car."

"He didn't *make* me sell it, Blue. It needed too much work. We couldn't afford to fix it."

I turned away, recalling our last ride in Mama's Nova. How the car smelled of Mama's perfume. How Star sat up front working the radio dial while I sat in back drawing in my sketchbook. A sadness filled me. I wanted that car back. I wanted Mama back. "Don't you miss driving?" I asked.

Mama squinted at me. "Why?"

I shrugged. "Just curious."

Mama studied Jinx's shed, like the answer was scratched in the rust. "I don't know, Blue. I'm really too busy to think about it."

"Oh, come on, Mama. Remember how it felt with the windows down and the breeze flapping through your hair?"

"All right, all right. . . ." Mama smiled. "I suppose I do."

I shifted my weight on the prickly grass. A twig snapped below me. "Can I ask you another question?"

"Okay."

"Why'd you marry Lyle?"

"Because I loved him, of course."

I reached for a second stick. I snapped that, too. I liked the sound, the brittle, quick snip. "Why?"

"Why do I love Lyle?"

I nodded.

"That's a funny question."

"Funny ha-ha or funny peculiar?"

"Funny peculiar. . . ."

I used my toe to drag another twig close. *Crack, snap.*

"Well," Mama started, "from the moment I met Lyle, he made me feel"—she blushed—"special. Like there was something about me he couldn't get enough of. No one ever made me feel that way before."

"Not even Pa?"

"It was different with your pa. We'd known each other forever, since grammar school. We were young when we got married, just eighteen. And your pa was so self-sufficient and independent. He didn't mind being alone. I used to wonder how he handled being in that rig all by himself for days on end with no one to talk to. But that was your pa. He didn't need a lot of words. He could say most anything with a look."

My eyelids grew heavy, hearing Mama conjure Pa like that.

"With Lyle," she continued, "he's different. If your pa was candlelight, I'd have to say Lyle would be a one-hundred-watt bulb." Mama laughed at the thought.

I searched for another stick.

"Your pa loved me, I never doubted that. And I loved him. More than he knew, I'm sure. But Lyle would fall apart without me. Lyle *needs* me."

I need you, too! I wanted to shout. *Star needed you!*

"Lyle's harder to describe."

Crack! Snap! Crack! Snap!

"What do you mean?" I asked.

"From the start, Lyle intrigued me. He was like a puzzle. One minute he'd be so sure of himself. The next his eyes would fill with tears and he'd reach for my hand and tell me he couldn't live without me. On our second date he said he loved me. That we were meant to be together. Day and night. Forever. . . ." A train clattered by, rattling the ground. I waited till it passed.

"I remember the first time Lyle hit you."

Mama pressed a finger to my lips. "Blue," she pleaded. "Don't, please."

I turned from her. "It was Star's and my first night sleeping in that horrid green bedroom Lyle'd informed us was *our room*. I felt like I was trapped inside a pitcher of lemon-lime Kool-Aid—"

"Blue, you should have said something. We could've painted it."

"Star was practicing her clarinet. I was drawing Pa's portrait. You two were in the next room. Fighting. We could hear you through the wall—"

"*All* couples argue, Blue. Your pa and I fought."

"I know," I said, recalling how Star and me would run for the creaky swing set out back, pumping hard, singing at the top of our lungs to drown them out. But by the time the lightning bugs flickered in the brush, the house would be quiet. We'd sneak back in, smiling at the sight of them nestled close on the divan.

Jinx and Mama's fights rarely had such happy endings. We learned that the night we heard the awful *wallop, thump* on the opposite side of the wall. Star and me made a vow right then and there, a promise we'd never call Lyle Pa. We cut a fat lock of hair off each other's head to prove our word was good. When Star left I combed the two pieces together, then braided her long red strands beside my ashy blond ones. That braid would never come undone. Neither would the promise woven into it.

"Maybe all couples argue," I said, "but not all husbands do what Lyle does to you."

Mama leaned on the dead trunk to stand. "It's too hot out here. I'm going in."

I grabbed her knee so hard I slapped her. "No. Wait."

"Blue, I've got a hundred things to do before work."

I stared at the red mark I left on her leg. "Why can't you tell Lyle to stop hitting you?"

"Shhh! The neighbors will hear."

"Like they haven't already!"

Mama took a deep breath and let it out. "I'm going in, Blue."

I stepped up onto the trunk of the dead dogwood. I was taller than her now. "Why do you let him do it?" Mama tried to get past. I held my arms out, blocking her. "*Tell* me."

"Blue, Lyle knows he has a problem with his temper. The two of us had a long talk about it after our last argument. He's promised me things will change." Mama touched my chin, attempting to turn my face toward hers. I didn't budge. "Blue, when a man makes a promise it's cruel to pull the rug out from under him. Especially when he's worked so hard to get to the point—"

"*What* point?"

"Lyle is genuinely sorry for his behavior, Blue. He knows what he's done in the past is unacceptable. He's asked me to work with him, to help him change. He wants to make amends."

"Like he did last night at the diner?"

"Blue, look at it this way—he may have blown up, but he didn't blow up at *me*."

"He dumped a table on us, for crying out loud!"

"Yes, but he got himself *out*. Before anyone got . . . hurt. That shows Lyle is trying. You've got to believe that, Blue. People deserve a second chance."

"Mama, he's had a second chance. And a third. And—"

"Blue, listen, he promised. This is the first time he *promised*!" Mama's eyes begged me to come along on the magic carpet ride.

There was a long silence. Mama was the first one to break it. "Will you promise me something, too?" she asked.

A small brown bird landed on Jinx's ratty hammock. He pooped in the middle and flew off. I stifled a smile. "What?"

"Promise me you'll try harder."

"Me?"

"Yes. Give Lyle a chance. Talk to him. Let him be a stepfather to you. And, Blue, it wouldn't hurt to let the little things slide."

"What's that supposed to mean?"

"Last night. At the diner. Lyle only brought up that bit about money because he's worried. They've been talking about layoffs at the plant."

"He called my teacher's present stupid!"

"He didn't mean anything by it. That's just his way, Blue."

My pulse pounded in my ears.

"Blue, what do you think? Can I count on you? Will you try? For *me*?"

Something inside me took over. I watched as my fingers curled. Uncurled. Inside me, the words ripped loose. *I want to shake you, Mama.*

My fingers knotted into fists. *I want to shake some sense into you.*

My fists trembled in front of me. My insides dared me. *Go ahead!*

Mama grabbed my wrists. "Blue?"

My head made a weird whirring noise. Like the projector in school when the film snaps and the picture screeches to a halt.

My hands fell to my sides. *How could I think such a thing? How could I think of hurting Mama? I gave Pa my word I'd look after her, that I'd take care of her.*

My fingers uncurled. The fire inside me smoldered. I stepped off the stump and stood close to Mama.

She looked down at my face. Into my eyes.

I laced my damp, shaky fingers through hers. "I'll try," I said, giving Mama that second promise she so desperately needed to hear. "You've got my word on it."

three

"Have you seen my peach uniform, Blue?"

I was sitting on the floor in front of Jinx's big box fan, my face pointed dead center as Mama stomped past. She has a way of walking heavy when she's hunting for something.

"Blue, I asked you a question."

The floorboards rattled against my behind. I pressed my face in closer to the fan. "Still in the ironing basket," I answered. My voice warbled through the spinning blades. I liked the sound so I said it again. Louder. "S-t-i-l-l i-n t-h-e i-r-o-n-i-n-g b-a-s-k-e-t."

"Okay, okay, I heard you the first time." More floor rattling. Mama slipped the uniform over the board. The skirt part hung like a curtain between us. She sprayed sizing up and down the front, and the mist landed on my shoulders. Mama ironed hard and fast, like she was fixing to do something a whole lot more serious than work a few wrinkles out of fabric.

I riffled through one of Mama's magazines. On the cover a small stone house with blue shutters was surrounded by flowers. Below it the caption read, "Plan your dream garden now."

Ha!

I looked up from the picture. "Mama, what time you working till tonight?"

The curtain Mama's uniform made lifted and fell. "It's hard to tell. Beau's got me on for a banquet." Banquets always meant leftovers, and it truly was the luck of the draw, as Pa used to say. Last time it was some sour stuff rolled in slimy cabbage that gave me diarrhea, but the time before that it was pizza. Mama set the iron upright. It made a noise like a hiccup. "Probably ten or so."

I counted out the hours. Four-thirty. Five-thirty. Six-thirty. Seven-thirty. Eight-thirty. Nine-thirty. Ten.

The fan flipped the magazine to a close-up picture of a tick, puffed up fat and shiny with the blood he'd sucked off some poor, unsuspecting mutt. "How to Detect a Tick: Ten Easy-to-Spot Warning Signs."

I held my finger in the page. "Do you think Lyle's coming back tonight?"

Mama collapsed the ironing board. "Your guess is as good as mine."

Mama went up to change.

I studied a makeup ad at the end of the tick article. A pretty girl stood in a field of wildflowers, her long wavy hair tossed by the breeze. Not dull straw hair like Mama's and mine, but gleaming golden-red hair like Star's. Shiny as the copper bottoms on Mama's pans. I squinted my eyes at the picture, trying to make the rest of her look like Star, too.

Mama's feet padded down the stairs. She stepped close, kissing the top of my head. She'd put on more of that skin-colored makeup. "There's goulash in the fridge, Blue. Remember—"

"I know, I know. Use the microwave oven, not the stove." A clump of hair fell loose from my ponytail. I pushed it back. "Mama?"

"Yeah, Blue?" Mama checked her watch. I heard the bus slow down then stop.

"Nothing. Just hurry home, okay?"

"I will," Mama said. "Now lock up behind me. The deadbolt, too. And don't forget to put the porch light on after supper."

Madame Safety. That's what Star and me'd nicknamed Mama. So it didn't make a dang bit of sense, how someone so prepared for an emergency could take up with the likes of Lyle Ethan Thorn.

I turned the deadbolt and watched Mama start down the sidewalk. Weeds poked through the narrow gray blocks. Mama's white sneakers mashed them down, but they popped right back. The grass was nearly to her knees. A dog could get ticks in there, easy.

Mama got on the bus. I watched it pull away. I stared at the empty space. My stomach knotted.

Jinx's cats ran to the door. They stood on their hind legs, their scrawny bodies stretched out long and lean as they scratched at the screen. I didn't let them in. Even with their ribs poking through their matted fur and their claws tangled in the crisscross mesh and that horrid cry that ripped a hole in my heart, still I turned my back on them.

I don't doubt it was pure craziness, what I was thinking. That if I could keep Jinx's cats away then maybe, just maybe, I could keep him away, too.

But I had to try.

❧

Upstairs, I stretched across my bed, staring at the girl in the makeup ad, pretending she was Star. I studied her face, watched her mouth the words "Where's Pa?" Her voice was invisible, like Pa's fishing line, but just as strong. "Where is he?"

In our old house Star and me had separate bedrooms. Star's was periwinkle, exactly like the crayon, and her walls were covered with posters. Nail polish bottles lined her dresser, bright as a string of Christmas lights. My room, across the hall, was pale yellow. One whole wall was covered with the wooden shelves Pa built for my art supplies and Nancy Drew books. My artwork was thumbtacked on the remaining walls: pencil portraits of Mama and Pa and Star, chalk drawings of Mama's flower garden, watercolor paintings of scenes I liked. My favorite painting, the one I'd hung front and center, won first place in the county fair art show in the ten-to-fourteen age group. I drew it looking at a page from a calendar Pa had tacked over his worktable in the garage. The day I noticed it I was sitting on a pile of tires, breathing in the familiar smells of turpentine and motor oil while Pa tinkered with Mama's Chevy Nova. "Is that anywhere around here?" I asked Pa. His greasy hand left a giant black thumbprint in the corner as he squinted at the picture. "Says here it's Hollerswallow Bridge and it's in Kentucky."

I sat there for the longest time, till my behind had fallen asleep on that pile of tires, staring at it, saying its name under my breath. The next day I made a sketch of Hollerswallow Bridge. I painted it in with watercolors. The sky was the best one I'd ever done. Darker blue up top, fading lighter toward the middle, with fluffy cotton-candy clouds.

It was Pa's idea to enter it into the contest. The day the fair opened we went to see it on display. A large blue ribbon was tacked to one corner. Mama took a picture of me standing beside it. Pa gave me a giant hug, and Star said I was going to be another Grandma Moses. Of all the things that happened that day—Pa winning me my pet goldfish, Little Ricky, Mama finding out her gladiolas took second place, and Star and me going on ride after ride till we could barely stand straight—it was the sight of that blue ribbon on my covered bridge that boomeranged through my heart the whole way home.

In our ugly lime-green bedroom, my bridge picture sat on my dresser, propped beside Little Ricky's glass bowl. I'd tried hanging it on the wall—four times in all, to be exact—but each time a train rattled by, knocking it to the floor.

My eyes wandered toward Star's dresser, to the framed picture of Pa—the last one ever taken of him—grinning, squinting into the sun, holding out a giant string of catfish. Beside it sat a green rock Star'd bought on account of claims it'd been found at the base of an Egyptian pyramid. Star was big on pyramids. She thought keeping it close to Pa's picture like that might help him in the afterlife. Off to the side, next to an unopened bag of M&M's, Star'd propped the broken pointer from her Ouija board. The plastic thing you set your fingers on while you're waiting for the words to get spelled out.

I remember the night it broke. Mama'd just started dating Jinx, who was still plain old Lyle at that point. It was after dinner. Mama'd made Swiss steak, his favorite. The two of them were having a beer, watching *Wheel of Fortune*. A woman with bright orange hair and a floppy chin shouted, "I want to buy a vowel!"

That's when Star got the idea of using the Ouija board to talk to Pa. "Come on," she said. "Let's go in the kitchen." She set everything up just so. Pa's picture was next to the board. The green rock was behind him. Star closed her eyes and rested her fingers on the edge of the plastic pointer. I copied her.

"We're trying to reach our pa," Star told the board. "Pa, it's Star and Blue. Can you hear us?"

I tried hard to block out the TV. A commercial came on, and two ladies talked about feminine protection. Thank God Star was busy concentrating 'cause under any other circumstances, that would've been a cue for her to ask, "Blue, you gotten yours yet?" Meaning my period, of course. And for the twelve zillionth time, I'd say, "No, I haven't, but why don't you check back again in another five minutes?"

"It's moving," Star whispered. "I felt it."

"Me too."

Star called out the letters. "B . . . L . . ." There was a long pause. "Okay, here we go . . . E . . . E . . . N . . . A . . . P."

We waited.

Star squinted at Pa's picture. "Bleenap? What's a bleenap, Pa?"

"Maybe it's a code," I said. "Or a foreign language."

Star shook her head. "Blue, think about it. Pa couldn't even do Pig Latin. *O-nay ay-way.*"

About that time, Jinx came strolling into the kitchen for two more cans of beer. The fridge light spilled across the table. "Well, well," he said, scratching his big head of hair. "Look what we got here. A *Ouija* board."

Jinx asked if he could try with us. And even though he hadn't done anything to make us sour on him yet, Star was real hesitant. Jinx convinced her, finally, by swearing his great-aunt Eudora from Altoona, Pennsylvania, had once been a highly sought-out fortune teller with a traveling circus.

Jinx parked himself at the head of the table, instructing us both on what to do. I turned the lights off and pulled the blinds while Star lit the lemon-scented candles we'd gotten Mama for Mother's Day. He asked to be alone with the Ouija board for a minute. To "connect his energies with it." Star seemed to know what he meant. She agreed.

We left the kitchen, waiting till he called us back.

"All right," he said finally. "Let's have a talk with Roy Hanson."

Candlelight bounced across Jinx's face as his fingers floated, just above the pointer. This time it slid all over. It said Pa wasn't dead at all. It said he was in Topeka, Kansas, except Topeka was spelled wrong. It said he had a good-paying job making toilet fixtures.

Star leapt up and danced around. "Pa's alive! Pa's alive!"

Jinx stretched over backward, laughing.

I turned the lights on and lifted the blinds. "What? What's so funny?"

My insides twisted as Jinx proudly pointed to the chunk of chewing gum he'd stuck to the needle on the bottom of the pointer. Why, he'd even had the nerve to use a piece of Pa's fishing line to bridge the space between the gum and his fingers.

Star's eyes narrowed. "How *could* you?" The Ouija board soared past the table and landed smack-dab in the middle of the living room, her kick was so good.

"Duck and cover!" Jinx yelled, still laughing as the plastic pointer soared one way and the needle—broken loose but still clinging to a three-inch length of Pa's fishing line and a wad of Jinx's gum—flew in another.

The plastic pointer was dusty now. I ran my fingers over its smooth edge, gazing into the see-through circle, which stared back like an open eye.

I checked the clock. Twenty to ten.

I sat on the edge of Star's bed, careful not to disturb any of the wrinkles I'd preserved since she left. I stared up at her newest poster, just over the headboard. A large fluorescent butterfly vibrated against a black velvet background. Below, in lavender letters, it said FREE. Sometimes, when Star couldn't sleep, she'd prop her pillows down on the foot end and lay there, backward, shining Pa's old flashlight on the poster. Even with my eyes closed I'd see the round glow, a full moon hovering just above my head as she whispered the word, "free . . . free," the sound of it rolling off her tongue like some exotic flavor she was imagining the taste of.

A ball of white light bounced across the wall.

Star? Oh, my God! Star?

It was Jinx's headlights. The sound of his truck, minus a muffler, rumbled down the driveway. Exhaust crept in through the open window.

I crossed the room, lifting the music box off my dresser. The gift from Pa that had waited for me in the bottom of that fancy shopping bag the night he won the money. I reached inside, feeling for the braid made from Star's and my hair. It was curled up small, like a sleeping snake. The money was hidden in there, too. The three thousand dollars. It was Mama's idea.

Jinx's truck door squealed open and slammed closed. The night was quiet again.

I miss you, Pa.

I wound the crank. I held it on my lap while "Blue Bayou" played, a song Pa had on a record by Roy Orbison. Every time he'd get to the word *blue,* Pa'd look straight at me and smile that magic smile of his.

I wound it again, feeling the notes speed up underneath my fingertips.

I miss you so much, Pa.

I listened till there was a wide space between each note. Finally, the silence took over. The last note played without my knowing.

The screen door walloped closed.

I pulled the top down and latched it.

I could hear Jinx wipe his boots on the mat inside the kitchen door. "C'mon, Miller! C'mon, Bud!" Jinx called his cats like Santa calling his reindeer, with the difference being, I suppose, that Santa didn't name the reindeer after favorite beers.

The electric can-opener buzzed in spurts. First for one can, then the other. Each of them—Bud and Miller both—got their own flavors 'cause of being so finicky.

Star used to say if you wanted to have any kind of opin-
ion at all in Jinx's house, you'd better start by changing
your name to something that comes in a tall, frosty bottle.
Sometimes, when we'd go grocery shopping with Mama,
we would wander down the beer aisle, trying on names.
"How about Heineken?" I asked her. "That's classy-
sounding." Star rolled her eyes. "Think about it, Blue.
You'd be nicknamed Heiny." Schlitz got voted down, too;
it sounded too much like something Mama'd lock us in
our room for saying.

Jinx turned the radio on in the kitchen, singing along.
I pictured him, the way his eyes grew wide when he tried
to hit the high notes.

I held my music box close.

Jinx's feet groaned on the stairs, his boots coming
down hard on each step. He stopped at the landing outside my door. I saw him through the crack. Waiting. His
teeth crunched down on something. I smelled winter-
green. He took a step forward. His knuckles tapped the
door. "Blue?"

I stood up so fast I felt dizzy.

"Blue?" He knocked again. The lamp from my room
lit up his face. He'd shaved. Combed his hair the way
Mama liked it. "Blue, I won't take but a minute of your
time."

Life Savers, that's what I smelled.

I gripped the doorknob and opened it. Just enough to fit Jinx's head, ear to ear. "Yeah?" I pressed the music box closer. A wooden corner poked my ribs.

Jinx stared at my chin. "What I wanted to say, Blue"— he chewed a piece of skin on the side of his thumb. I noticed he'd cleaned his nails. "What I wanted to say was, uh, what I did at the diner last night, getting upset, spilling that food all over your mama and you, well, I— I'm *sorry* for it."

Jinx cleared his throat. I could tell from the phlegm rattling around that he had a big old hawker in there. Star used to say how Mama and me were going to find her dead of embarrassment the next time he spit one out his pickup truck window.

I tried to think what to say.

I saw Mama's face in my mind. *Give Lyle a chance, Blue. . . . Will you try?*

"Blue?" Jinx swallowed, his Adam's apple leaping up high and swooping back down. The rattling was gone.

Mama's eyes begged me. *Blue? For me?*

I forced myself to look at his face. He looked tired. Worn out. "Okay," I said. "I accept your apology."

Jinx fixed his eyes on the floor. He backed into the shadows. "Thanks, Blue," he mumbled. "Thanks."

I said something Pa used to say: "Don't mention it."

I pushed the door closed, thinking of something else he'd said: that life is a lot like a poker game. You've got to know when to hold on to the hand you got dealt and play it out and, likewise, when you'd best throw it in and run for the hills.

See, Pa, it doesn't mean anything, my being nice to Jinx. This is the hand we got dealt, and Mama's still holding. Trying to get me to hold, too.

I touched my face to the music box, feeling its cool top on my hot cheek. I kissed it before I put it back.

She's a gambler, Pa. . . .

I reached in my sock drawer for the key to lock it.

. . . Just like you were.

four

The next morning the kitchen smelled of fresh flowers and perked coffee. An open envelope with Mama's name printed in large careful letters leaned against a ball of crumpled gift wrap.

"Mama?" I called, raising my voice over the eight-track playing on Jinx's stereo. "Where are you?"

"Out here!" she called back.

I followed her voice. Mama was stretched out on the webbed chaise lounge, watching Jinx's feet poke out from underneath his truck. She had on what Star and me'd nick-named her Smile Pretty dress on account of Mama always wearing it after her and Jinx made up. A new chain hung from her neck. A gold heart locket shimmered against the bright green fabric. She caught me eyeing her from behind the screen door. "Come on out," she said, smiling.

Ready, Pa? Here we go again. The reappearance of the New, Improved Lyle Ethan Thorn.

"Whatcha doing?" I asked, leaning on the arm of her chair. I could hear Jinx's music through the open window.

"Lyle's got the day off," Mama answered. "He's fixing his muffler."

His hairy arm popped out from underneath the truck, tapping Mama's ankle. "Toss me that clamp, Ceil?"

Mama leaned forward, pressing the metal U into Jinx's hand. The cart rolled away. "Did you see the pretty carnations Lyle brought me?" she asked.

I stared at the black fingerprint he'd left on her ankle. "Yeah," I said. "I saw them." I hated carnations. They smelled like a funeral.

Mama twirled a strand of my hair around her finger till it pulled tight. "I hear Lyle apologized to you," she whispered. "And I hear you accepted it." A blond wisp dangled off her diamond. "That means a lot to me, honey."

I faked a smile, thinking of the time Star told Mama she'd *never* accept one of Jinx's apologies, saying how they'd proved to be about as helpful as a tent in a tornado.

Jinx rolled out from under the truck, his neck spotted with scabs where he'd cut himself shaving. He kissed Mama, then turned to me. "Hi, Blue," he said, grinning. "How's things?"

I stared at my feet. "Fine, thanks."

"Good," he said. "Hop in. Let's the three of us go for a

ride. Try out the new muffler." Jinx hurried toward the cab, holding the passenger-side door open. "I know, we'll go for ice cream. How's that sound?"

Mama beamed like she'd been crowned Queen of Someplace Fancy. "That sounds like fun," she said, sliding in, clear to the middle. "Blue," she yelled back, patting the empty space beside her, "doesn't that sound fun to you?"

The morning sun was hot on my neck. My stomach growled. I hadn't had breakfast yet. "Yeah," I mumbled, hopping in. "Sure does."

Jinx took what Mama calls "the scenic route." His tires grabbed up gravel, scattering it into the sprawling sea of green on both sides of us. Mama squinted down the dry sun-bleached road, her head bouncing when the truck bounced.

Jinx's lighter popped. The orange glow floated toward the tip of his cigarette. The skin on his face pulled tight while he puffed. Ashes fluttered through the cab. One landed in Mama's hair. I watched to make sure it went out.

It was quiet. An itchy, nervous quiet. I stuck my head out the window, ignoring the road dust burning my eyes. My lips dried out. I licked them, leaned out farther. The wind pushed on my face. I pushed back. Harder. *Harder.* Till I got the whoosh in my stomach I was after—that feeling of having all my insides scooped out and put back clean.

Udderly Good Soft Serve, managed by some Ralph
guy Jinx knew from the cheese factory, was plunked in the
middle of nowhere. Every inhale reeked of cow manure.

Jinx stepped to the window and shook Ralph's hand.
"How ya doing, buddy? I got the family with me today."

Family, my foot.

"What'll it be for you fine folks?" Ralph asked, spit
hissing through his teeth.

I stepped back from the window and pretended to read
the Thursday specials while my forehead dried out.

Mama shot Ralph her Smile Pretty dress smile and
ordered a single scoop of raspberry sherbet. Jinx got a
triple scoop of something green and bumpy. I asked for a
double scoop of Udderly Good Soft Serve's flavor of the
day, Moo Moo Marble Crunch.

Jinx picked a picnic table close to the road. He sank his
teeth in the ice cream, leaving deep tracks in the green
lumps. Mama sat next to him, taking long, steady licks
like Miller and Bud do when they clean themselves.

I sat on the other side. A rig barreled by, one like Pa
used to drive. I leaned forward, waiting for the feel of its
thunder in my ribs, but it roared by too fast.

Three girls around Star's age rode toward us on ten-
speed bikes. The two blond ones moved in unison like

the Doublemint Twins as they slowed up, using their hands like visors to gaze at the giant plastic cone jutting from the roof.

The third girl had long red hair. She stopped pedaling and coasted till she was barely moving, wiggling the handlebars so the front tire wavered from side to side, holding her up till she had to either put a foot down or fall. The only other person I'd ever seen do that was Star.

I watched as her sandal touched the pavement. She yelled something to the twins. All three dug in their pockets, counting change.

The red-headed girl pushed her hair out of her face. She had Star's pointy chin. "I don't have enough," she called. "How about you two?"

The twins shook their heads and pedaled off, but the red-haired girl stayed put, her freckled arm bent across her forehead. Star had freckles on her arms, too. Pa used to say it looked like she got a suntan through a screened door.

I stopped breathing. She was staring in *my* direction.

Cripes, I thought, *what if it is Star? What if all that talk about ice-cream money was just a ploy, something to buy time after spotting me?*

My ice cream was melting down my arm.

The twins were way ahead. One of them yelled back. "Are you *coming*?"

Something inside pushed me. A hot spark, crackling. Ice cream splattered my ankle as I jumped up, dropping my cone.

The spark snapped into a flame, propelling me. Just like a human cannonball, I flew straight toward the red-haired girl.

Star, come back! I need you! I can't make it without you!

A car horn blasted. A man yelled out his window. "Hey, kid! Get out of the road!"

A dark blur shot past. "Star! Wait!" I screamed, waving, jumping. My feet smacked hard on the just-paved road. I gasped for air, sucking in the hot tar smell. "Star, don't go!"

Mama's hand clenched my arm. I pulled loose.

Another car. Another horn.

She grabbed again. Pulled harder. We both fell back onto the gritty shoulder. "Blue, what are you *doing*?"

I yanked my arm away, fixing my gaze on the girl as she hopped on her bike. Her feet moved in small, fast circles. Down the dusty road. Past a field of corn.

Gone. She was gone.

I clutched Mama's shoulders. "Did you *see* her?" I yelled. "Did you?"

Mama touched my face, bringing it forward so our foreheads touched. "I know," she whispered. "I know. You're not the only one who misses her."

I rested my head on Mama's shoulder on the ride back, staring at the magnet of Jesus on Jinx's dashboard, noticing how his eyes seemed to follow me.

Jinx put his signal on, turning down our street. His foot slammed hard on the brakes, and we lunged forward. "Lyle, what—?" Mama started, reaching for the dashboard.

The truck stalled out. The car in back of us swerved, blasting its horn.

The muscles in Jinx's jaw pulled tight. His eyes opened wide, floating like two pennies in a bowl of milk.

Mama grabbed his arm, leaving marks where her nails dug in. "Lyle, what *is* it?"

Jinx pushed the clutch and turned the key, pulling in the driveway, still staring over his shoulder. I undid my seat belt, following his eyes to the dark shadow clinging to the side of the road.

"Lyle," Mama pleaded, "tell me what's wrong!"

Jinx's door flew open.

Mama and me hopped out, following.

Two houses down, Miller's thin gray body was stretched out, long and limp. Blood seeped from his head, collecting in a shiny red puddle.

Jinx knelt beside him, resting his hand on Miller's chest. He rocked forward, heaving as he choked out the words, "Someone hit my cat, Ceil. . . . Someone killed my Miller."

Mama gripped his shoulder, her nails going white when she squeezed and pink when she let up. White, pink, white, pink, in rhythm to Jinx's swaying. "Let's get him out of the road," she said.

Jinx worked his hands underneath the dead cat. He walked toward the side of the house, Miller spilling off both sides of his spread fingers.

Mama trailed behind, then me. Like a funeral parade.

I heard a yowl. The skin on my arms prickled. I glanced ahead at Miller, still as stone, then up at Star's and my bedroom window, where Bud sat on the sill, watching us. I figured he *had* to know. Miller and him were from the same litter. And kin have that thread that runs through their hearts, holding them together like squares on a quilt, no matter what.

Jinx stopped at the trash can. His face was splotchy from crying. "Lift that lid for me, Ceil?"

"Oh, Lyle, come on. Don't you think we should bury him?"

Jinx itched his chin on his shoulder, and Miller swooped sideways. "No, I don't. Crazy animals'll dig him up. Gnaw at him, piece by piece."

Mama sighed, lifting the lid off the gray can. The smell pushed the ice cream back into my throat.

Flies buzzed around the edge. I stared at the garbage like I was seeing it for the very first time. An empty toothpaste tube leaning on a napkin full of melon seeds. Jinx's cereal box, wedged between a banana peel and an empty Budweiser bottle. A plastic bag leaking dirty cat litter. A hundred cigarette butts, bent into tiny golden *L*s.

I stepped backward—into the yard of the lady Jinx called Madame Busybody—till I could see past the sagging roof and into the window Bud perched in. His green eyes were on me. He mashed his face on the screen and cried out again, a long, hungry yowl.

Jinx laid Miller across the trash. "Bye, Miller. My main man. I'm gonna miss you."

Mama lowered the lid.

A dark circle floated over Miller, like the moon eclipsing the sun.

five

That night, for the first time in the whole entire year of living at Jinx's house, Bud slept on my bed.

I was lying awake, watching the car lights slide across the ceiling boards when Bud climbed on my chest and stared me down with those glow-in-the-dark eyes of his. Star'd always said cats were psychic, and with the sight of Bud spooking me good, I wasn't doubting it one bit.

It was plenty clear. Bud was sending me a message.

I threw a shirt on over my nightgown, crept downstairs, and slipped out the back door. The grass was damp on my bare feet. The moon hung like a cereal bowl tipped sideways over the black trees. I moved my hand along the chain link fence, feeling my way to the shed.

The shovel leaned on the wall, just inside the door. The handle was rough. Jinx didn't oil it like Pa used to. Its wide, dry cracks pressed on my hands, and my heel ached, straining against the cold metal. I jabbed the hard ground. A sliver shot into my palm. I licked the wet off my upper lip. Again, I plunged. Hit rock. Another sliver. A hot pain raged the length of my thumb. I dug and dug till the hole was deep enough.

Miller was cool in my warm arms. He didn't lop over anymore. I lowered him into the hole. The moon glimmered on his short gray fur, making it look silver.

"You'll be okay here," I told him, covering him up with the shirt I'd grabbed. "I'll keep an eye on Bud. Don't you worry about that." I filled his grave with dirt, patting it flat, leaving my hand there while I finished what I had to say. "And don't pay any mind to what Jinx said, either—about crazy animals coming after you. He *would* say that, wouldn't he? Takes one to know one."

I put the shovel back and closed the shed. I made a little cross out of sticks, shoved it into the loose earth, and went back inside.

Bud was still on my bed, waiting for a report.

"It's taken care of," I whispered. "Your brother's in his resting place. A *decent* resting place."

Bud settled down next to me, just like he understood. I scratched his head till a thick purr rattled deep in his throat, and we both fell back to sleep.

The phone woke me up. I could hear Jinx answer it in his and Mama's room. "Yeah? Who's this?"

I checked the clock. Twenty after five. It was just getting light out.

"Goddamnit, who *is* this?" Jinx yelled, losing what little patience he had. He slammed the phone down hard—right after he got done telling whoever it was to go straight to hell and stay there.

It happened again around six. *Ring, ring. Go to hell. Slam.*

I couldn't go back to sleep. Bud followed close while I went down to pee, then he trailed me into the kitchen.

Mama was sitting in the dim morning light. She had Jinx's robe on. It brought his smell into the room along with her. "Morning, Blue."

"Morning, Mama." I poured myself a tall glass of apple juice and sat across from her. "Couldn't sleep?" I caught a look at my feet, plastered with dried mud, and curled them behind the cold metal chair rungs.

"No. Neither could Lyle. He's just now dozing some. He kept dreaming about that dead cat. He'd go to sleep, have a nightmare, go to sleep, have a nightmare. . . ." She sipped her coffee. "Poor Lyle."

"Poor *Miller,*" I added, not wanting her to forget it was *him,* after all, who got his brains smashed out. "And poor Bud, too, getting left all alone like that."

Bud rubbed against my shin like he'd heard me. I reached under the table, digging his small, hard head with my stubby nails. I felt a bump near his ear. I hoped it wasn't a tick.

The sun squeezed in through the blinds over the sink, spilling long, dark stripes across the plastic tablecloth.

Mama'd propped a fancy peach-colored envelope against the bowl of fake fruit. LYLE, it said, in big black letters. His name was underlined six or seven times, and little hearts were drawn all around it, except none of their tops connected, so they looked more like *V*s with their loopy ends caving into the middle. Mama always said she couldn't draw to save her soul, and looking at those hearts, I was inclined to believe her.

"What's the card for?" I asked.

The steam from her coffee rose up. She reminded me of the Wizard of Oz, with her face looming in the vapor.

"It's for Lyle," she said.

"Mama, I know *who* it's for. It says so right there. L-Y-L-E. Swimming in a sea of hearts. At least, I *think* they're hearts."

Mama leaned forward. Her shadow shifted, sprawling across the thin, dark table stripes. It looked like she was in prison. "Yes, Blue. They're hearts. And you don't have to get all snippy-sounding."

The air was close. I peeled my arms off the tablecloth, sure some of my skin was going to stick there when I did. "So," I asked, "what's the special occasion?"

Mama touched the edge of the envelope. "It's our first wedding anniversary. June eighteenth. Remember?"

I couldn't forget if I wanted to. My mind flashed a picture of the reception: Jinx dancing Mama across the dirty wood floor of Duffy's Tavern, peanut shells crunching below their feet while Star and me pumped coins in the jukebox and ate pickled kielbasa off the bar till our tongues felt like they'd been pickled, too. We weren't saying one word about the wedding. Almost like it hadn't happened.

I felt Mama's eyes on me, waiting for me to say something. Like *congratulations,* maybe.

I lucked out. The phone rang.

Mama dove at it, not wanting to disturb Jinx. "Hello?" A long thread hung off the robe, trailing her like a tail. "Hello?" She waited. "Look, whoever you are, please don't call back again unless you've got something to say." Mama set the phone down soft. Her shadow slid back behind the jail bars. "That happened earlier. Twice."

"I know," I said. "I heard it." A rip in the chair pad pinched my thigh, but Bud was asleep on my foot, so I tried not to move. "You working today?"

"Not today. Beau switched the schedule for me."
Mama grinned. "Lyle planned a little surprise for our
anniversary."

"A surprise? Like what?"

"Lyle's taking me on a trip."

"A *trip*? What kind of trip?"

Jinx never took Mama anywhere. Unless you count
the time before Star left when the four of us drove to
Albany, New York, to pick up a load of Canadian cheese
Jinx's foreman sent him after. Mama had a picture hanging in the living room that Jinx took of her and Star and
me in front of the state capitol building. Right after, we
had lunch—hot dogs a vendor was selling nearby. Star
asked for sauerkraut, something she never should've done
because of it not agreeing with her. She threw up the
whole way home. Out the window, down the highway,
all along Interstate 90.

Mama pulled a newspaper clipping out of Jinx's robe
pocket. "'Get away from it all in sunny South Yarmouth,'"
she read. "'Clean, spacious, air-conditioned accommoda-
tions. Free phone and cable TV in every room. Private
balcony overlooking the majestic beaches of Cape Cod.'"
Mama handed me the ad. "Pretty nice, huh?"

I knew this was my cue to start gushing about how
wonderful it sounded. "Yeah," I said. "Terrific." But my

voice was as flat and colorless as the ad. I folded it once, sticking it between the two plastic bananas.

Mama didn't exactly hide her disappointment. I felt guilty. Not just 'cause I didn't gush and fuss, but 'cause I really *couldn't* find it in myself to be happy for her.

Mama leaned forward to touch my hand. "This is important to me, Blue. I know Lyle and I have had our share of troubles, but this is a chance for us to wipe the slate clean, to start over." She gave my hand a pat, then sat back, cross-legged.

I felt a chip on the edge of my juice glass. I ran my finger across it till my skin snagged. "When are you leaving?"

"Tomorrow morning. Saturday."

Her answer kicked the air out of my lungs. "*Tomorrow?* But that's so soon!"

Mama poured more coffee. "That's exactly what I said—'Lyle, my goodness, there's barely time for me to pack!'"

My fingers felt rubbery. I pressed them against the glass's raw edge.

Pa was the first to leave. Then Star. Now Mama.

I pressed harder. The pain gave me something to concentrate on while my mind spun. Quick, dizzy circles like we danced in our last night with Pa. "But, Mama," I started. "You never went off and *left* me before. What if something happens?"

"Oh, Blue. . . ." Mama scruffed my hair like I was some stupid two-year-old. "Nothing's going to happen."

I pulled away, smoothing my bangs back. I was about to say "Promise?" when I caught myself. Talk about two-year-olds. "When are you coming back?" I asked instead.

"Sunday night. Beau and Aggie said you can sleep at their place tomorrow."

I pictured myself curled up on the dark, itchy sofa in the skinny tin living room of Beau and Aggie's mobile home, all nine of their cats perched on the high back glaring down at me. Eighteen glow-in-the-dark eyes sending me a psychic message—that Mama'd disappeared. I saw myself sinking. Buried in a grave of broken springs and smelly cat pee.

"C—Can I stay here instead?" I asked. "I mean, I'll be thirteen in two weeks."

"Three."

"Yeah, well, three. Still, can I?"

I pushed my finger down harder on the glass's chipped edge, on that tiny little *V.* A bright red drop of blood trickled down the length of my finger, landing in the valley of skin connecting it to my thumb.

Mama didn't notice. "Tell you what," she said, patting my shoulder, walking past. "I'll talk it over with Lyle."

six

I made a marker for Miller's grave by cutting up one of Jinx's beer cartons and taping the word *Miller* to a Styrofoam tray I found in the kitchen pail. I sat beside it, eating a cherry Popsicle, reading an article on adoption in one of Mama's magazines. Just in case Mama vanished like Pa and Star, and Beau and Aggie decided to take pity on me and call me their own. I got a chill clear through me when I realized what my new name would be: *Blue Silver.*

On the way back to the house, I noticed a fallen bird's nest leaning against the tire of my rusty bike. It made me think of a time when I was little, riding on Pa's shoulders, and spotted a nest wedged in the crook of our peach tree. Pa stepped close so I could see inside.

"Where's Mama?" I gasped, pointing at the lonely blue eggs.

Mama, not knowing I was asking about the bird, hurried over. "Mama's right here," she said, lifting me off Pa's shoulders, hugging me to her.

Mama was running the vacuum when I came in. She had the kitchen table loaded with stuff for the trip— tanning oil, sunglasses, two new tube tops, a paperback novel, a wide-brimmed straw hat, Pa's binoculars, a bottle of peach nail polish, and two pairs of neon yellow flip-flops, size eight and size twelve, with the price tags still on them.

I poured some apple juice. Bud ran over and mashed his face against my ankles.

Mama pulled the plug on the vacuum. "Looks like you've got yourself a new friend."

I shrugged and sat down, fiddling with the strap on Pa's binoculars. The magazine slipped off my knee, scaring Bud away. I stared down at the page it'd fallen open to. Some fancy-schmancy hotel ad. A man and a woman were walking on the beach at sunset. The ocean lapped at their bare feet. The sun was a huge golden ball, ready to roll them down like bowling pins.

Mama snipped the plastic string on the flip-flops. "Hey, Miss Smarty Pants, what's that you're reading?"

I stared at the woman in the picture, holding my big toe over the spot where her hand held his.

Leave, lady. Leave while you've got the chance.

"Nothing," I said, and picked it up.

Mama sat across from me. She shook her nail polish and undid the top. The smell made my apple juice taste funny. I watched her brush on the polish—exactly the opposite of how Star did it—starting with her baby toe, working her way up. "So, Blue, what would you like me to bring you?"

"Huh?"

"You know, from Cape Cod. For a souvenir."

I flipped the page. *Betsy Sanders from Jackson Hole, Wyoming, shares her secret bran muffin recipe. "Eating plenty of fiber helps my busy corporate executive husband avoid constipation," Betsy began.*

"How about a stuffed animal? Or a T-shirt? What size are you now?" Mama's eyes dropped to my chest, to the two small bumps she hadn't mentioned noticing. "Ladies small? Medium?"

She stared, waiting for my answer. I felt my throat close. "Medium's good," I croaked, then started coughing.

Mama's toenails glistened like a row of shiny shells. "Drink some juice," she said, sliding my glass closer. "That always helps me."

Mama and Jinx had enough stuff packed in the back of that old black pickup truck to run off for good. I tried not to see it as an omen.

Jinx's beer cooler went in last. I watched from the window as he informed Mama that Miller was the only beer in the world he'd ever drink again, as a tribute to his dear departed cat.

Jinx tied a tarp over the top.

Mama clumped toward the house. (She always did walk funny in heels.) She was wearing an ugly green dress Jinx had bought her, just a tad darker than her Smile Pretty dress. Jinx was big on lime-green. Star claims it's because of him being composed of 100 percent pure bile himself.

Mama opened the fridge door and popped the top on a Pepsi Light. "Come on over here, Blue." She waved her arm like Carol Merrill on *Let's Make a Deal,* showing off the prizes behind Door Number Three. She pointed to an unopened carton of chocolate milk, then held up a brown box from Jinx's cheese factory, containing one dozen packages of individually wrapped string cheese. My favorite. "Lyle got this for you all by himself," she said. "I didn't even ask him to. That was thoughtful, wasn't it?"

I was so relieved about Mama and him not making me stay with Beau and Aggie, I'd have agreed to Jinx being named president of the United States. "Yeah, Mama."

She opened the freezer next. A burst of frosty gray air tumbled out. "I bought you two TV dinners. One for tonight, one for tomorrow night. I picked the kinds you like, the ones with desserts." She smiled. I smiled back. The final items on the food tour were a box of day-old doughnuts, two cans of ravioli, and a bag of cheese curls for a TV snack.

"I'll call you tonight," she said, standing in the doorway. "Right after we get settled in. Now, lock up behind me. Don't let anybody in. There's extra litter for Bud under the sink and—*oh*—don't forget to pull the blinds when the sun goes down. Leave a couple lights on downstairs when you go up to bed. And if you need anything—"

"I know, I know. Call Beau and Aggie."

"Right." Mama kissed my forehead. I let the damp spot sit there instead of wiping it away, even though it tickled. "You be careful," she said. "You be careful, Baby Blue."

Her calling me that gave me the same fat lump in my throat it always did. I crossed my arms over my chest to keep my heart from leaping out right there in front of her. "I will," I said. "You be careful, too."

I watched from the window while Mama walked around the side of the house to the driveway, where Jinx waited in the truck.

I touched my nose to the window screen. "*Psssst . . .* Mama . . . I forgot to tell you something."

Mama's heels scrubbed the driveway as she wobbled toward the window. "What is it, Blue?"

"Guess what I did."

"What do you mean, *'Guess what I did'*?"

"The night before last. While you were sleeping. Guess what I did."

Mama looked over her shoulder at Jinx—sitting up high in his truck, puffing on a cigarette—then back at me. "Blue, is this some kind of—"

"I buried Miller. Out back."

Mama squinted through the screen at me. "You *what?*"

"I buried Miller. You know, Miller the cat?"

"I know who Miller is. *Was.* I mean, why? Why'd you bury him?"

"'Cause, Mama, he was *dead.*"

"That's not what I mean."

"He deserved better, Mama." I swallowed hard. "You shouldn't say you *love* something one minute then lay it out like trash the next."

Mama was silent for a long moment. "How'd I ever get so lucky?" she said softly.

"Huh?"

"Getting a daughter like you. You're sensitive and talented and smart and—"

I knew *pretty* wasn't coming next. Pa used to call Star and me "Beauty and the Brains." You can guess which one I was. "Thanks," I said.

". . . And pretty."

"Oh, Mama, I am *not.*" I was blushing up a storm.

"You are too. It's just hard for you to see right now. You're at that age. Everything's trying to catch up with everything else. But you'll see. One day you'll wake up and find yourself smiling at your own reflection. And it won't be just prettiness you'll see in that mirror either, because you've got what it takes on the inside to make the outside truly shine." She sighed, picking at a rip in the screen mesh.

"Mama?"

"There's so much I admire about you, Blue." Her finger slipped through the hole. She pulled it back, smoothing the wiry threads into place. "Your sister, too. I should have told her that more before she—"

"You'll get the chance," I interrupted. I wasn't sure I believed it.

Mama's eyes were glassy-looking. "I do hope so."

I said it again. "You'll *get* the chance." Maybe I did believe it.

Mama forced a smile.

Jinx clicked on the radio in his truck. A song began, and he cranked it up, tapping out the rhythm on his steering wheel.

"I'd better go," Mama said.

I felt guilty wishing what I did—that she'd change her mind and stay—but I wished for it anyway.

Mama put a kiss on her finger and brought it to the screen, pressing till the mesh gave. I touched my finger to hers. She kept it there a second, then let go. Her heels scraped back toward the truck.

I looked away till I heard the door close.

Mama hung her head out the window, waving.

Jinx backed out.

The breeze lifted Mama's hair, tossing it around like pale wheat under clear skies.

I memorized her just that way. Smiling. Waving. Leaving kisses on the window for me. I memorized every detail of my mama, Cecilia Hanson Thorn. Every last detail.

Just in case.

part two

seven

I pulled the string inside Star's and my closet. The bare lightbulb gobbled up the darkness. In one corner I'd stacked the gifts for future artists I'd outgrown: a Spirograph set, an Etch-A-Sketch, a loom to make potholders, a beaded jewelry kit. In another, leaning against Star's old pogo stick, was the bright orange hula hoop I remembered getting on my eighth birthday. Star, who was eleven at the time, was pogo-sticking her way up and down our driveway. I was close by, swinging my hips, giddy with the *shugga-shugga-shoooooop* sound the hoop made. Pa stepped off the back porch, looking up from the daily paper. Smiling, he said, "Well, if it ain't Miss Round-and-Round and Miss Up-and-Down."

I knew the inside of our closet by heart. Just like I knew every single solitary item Star took with her: her black Frye boots, three gauze shirts, and both her favorite skirts—the tie-dyed one with the fringe and the crinkly black one with the little white patterns stamped all over.

I'd always said the shapes looked like wide-open mouths with rotten teeth, but Star'd informed me the pattern was *abstract,* meaning a person's mind sees what it wants to see. And if it turns out to be something weird, like bad teeth, then that says something about the person, not the design.

Star knew a lot about that kind of stuff, what makes people tick. All 'cause of who she'd been in a past life, long before she became Star Hanson. At least, that's what Madame Beauregard at the Second Annual Psychic Fair at the downtown Valley Inn told her. She said Star'd been a spiritual adviser to royalty many lifetimes ago.

"Where?" Star asked her.

Madame Beauregard answered in a trance. Star claims her eyes rolled back in her head so far she looked like she was going to have a seizure. "Someplace foreign," she answered. "It's warm there. Someplace that begins with the letter *E. . . .*"

Star bugged me the whole next day. "Where could it be, Blue? Ethiopia? Egypt? Ecuador?"

"How about England?"

"You're a big help," she snapped. "They speak English in England. Does that sound foreign to you?"

What used to be Star's favorite shirt hung on a nail inside our closet. The white gauzy one with the row of purple flowers stitched down the front. I worked my fingers inside the jagged burn hole Jinx's cigarette had put on the right sleeve, like touching it could erase the memory of Star yelling, "Don't you hit our mama!" Those were her exact words. I remember every detail of what happened that night, and with good reason: It was the last time I saw my sister.

Star'd turned sixteen the day before. Her leftover birthday cake sat in the middle of the table. Mama'd spelled out her name using chocolate chips. When Pa was alive, we had a ritual: Whoever had a birthday got to decide where we'd eat supper. Pa always picked the Thunderbird Drive-In 'cause they had a zillion Elvis songs in their jukebox, and Mama and Star, who seldom agreed on anything, both favored a restaurant in town that Pa said smelled like boiled socks. I liked Shorty's Barbecue. I'd call first picks and lead the way toward my favorite booth. Star would roll her eyes and call me a "boring stick-in-the-mud," but I'd ignore her, taking pleasure in watching everybody follow me. I liked things being the same.

At Jinx's house, birthdays were nothing special. I'd set the table for dinner exactly how I'd set it every other night since Lyle had become Jinx—with the barn scene on Mama's blue-and-white plates facing everybody but him. His barn I'd turned upside down.

That particular evening, my eyes roamed over the *A* and *R*—the only two letters left on Star's cake—the whole time Jinx moaned about Mama forgetting to buy ketchup for his fish sticks. Must be Mama got tired of hearing it. She wiped her mouth on her napkin, pushed her chair in like she was done—except she wasn't—and walked out the door.

Jinx's jaw dropped. Star and I stared at our plates. We sat there, still as statues and just as quiet, too. Mama came back a half hour later, her hair stuck flat to her head with sweat.

Jinx's neck got dark and rashy and, like a thermometer, the red climbed upward till his whole face filled in. His fingers drummed the table. "Where you been, Ceil?"

Mama didn't answer. She opened a small grocery bag and produced a bottle of ketchup, setting it beside Jinx's plate. Pressing her napkin on her lap, she went back to cutting her lettuce in neat, even squares, sliding each off the fork with her teeth, real ladylike. We all watched till the last square was gone.

Jinx reached in his shirt pocket for a cigarette. He tapped it on the table before lighting it. "You should've said where you were going, Ceil. It ain't polite, up and leaving in the middle of a meal like that."

Mama placed her napkin in the middle of her plate.

I realized I hadn't breathed in a while. I sucked in air. It made me cough. Star refilled my lemonade, and I drank it down so fast my teeth ached from the cold.

Jinx puffed on his cigarette, blowing smoke out his nose. He looked just like a bull getting ready to charge. "I'm *talking* to you, Ceil."

Mama looked up. "I believe you made it quite clear your meal was unsatisfactory." She opened the ketchup and squeezed a fat dollop on Jinx's uneaten fish sticks. "There," she said, flashing a phony smile. "Enjoy."

I watched Jinx's hands, one on each side of his plate. How his fingers stretched out and pulled back into huge, knotty fists.

He lunged across the table at Mama. She jumped up as Jinx grabbed her chair. He landed face-first on the dingy kitchen tile. Noises crept from his throat. Sounds like an animal's growl.

"Mama!" Star yelled. "Go hide!"

Mama darted toward the living room.

Star stretched herself across the door frame between the two rooms. The string on the ceiling light swung behind her head. The round, white light glowed like a halo. Jinx toyed with her, sticking his face in and out of the open spaces her shifting body made. She pushed her face into his. "Don't you hit our mama!"

Jinx's cigarette dangled from his lip. His rough, scratchy laugh rocked its red tip. Ashes flew everywhere. One landed on Star's long sleeve. The white fabric sparked. I smelled gauze burning. Star screamed, and I ran toward her, swatting at the tiny flame.

Jinx pushed past. He pinned Mama to the floor, his hands clamped around her neck. Chokes squeaked from her pinched throat.

I leapt at him from behind, grabbing on to his thick hair. I tried to pry him loose, but he shrugged me off. Effortlessly. I toppled backward and took a lamp down with me.

Mama cried as Jinx smacked her head against the floor.

Star ran to the phone. Pressing the receiver to her shoulder with her chin, she bit her lip, drawing her arm out of the singed sleeve. I stared at the puckery swell of her scorched skin while she dialed.

&

Jinx kicked the footstool over on his way to the kitchen. "You did it again, Ceil! You went and made me lose my temper." I heard the top on a beer pop open. The transistor radio came on.

Mama sat curled in a corner of the living room. I clicked on the one lamp that hadn't gotten busted and she cringed, like the light was striking at her, too. "Come on, Mama," I said. "Let me see your face."

Mama held her palm out. "I'll be fine. Leave me alone."

I'd packed ice in a dish towel. I knelt beside her, tugging

her arms from the front of her face. Her bottom lip was bleeding. One of her eyes was puffy.

Dang, Pa, it's happened again.

Finally, Mama let me press the ice against her face. Gently, like always. Her head lopped sideways. I could feel its full weight on my shoulder as her body shook and she cried in small, silent sobs.

Star's smelly burned sleeve swung at her side as she paced the living room, dodging the debris.

Headlights splashed across the windows. All three of us froze.

A car door slammed closed. A knock came at the door.

Star answered it. Two policemen stood in the entryway. One was tall with long blond sideburns. The second was dark-haired, shorter.

Mama jumped up fast, her ice cubes scattering.

The shorter officer stepped toward her. "You're hurt," he said. "What's going on here?"

"Nothing. I—" Mama looked down, seeing for the first time what a shambles the room was in. She shook her head. "It—it's not what you think."

Jinx called from the other room. "Who's that you're talking to, Ceil?" The radio clicked off and he appeared in the doorway, shoveling a handful of Beer Nuts in his mouth. "Well . . . gentlemen." He tipped his Budweiser bottle forward as if to toast them. "Care for a cold one?"

The blond policeman stepped toward Jinx.

Mama rushed forward to block his path. "Wait! I can explain everything. There's been a misunderstanding! Please, don't!"

The second cop moved past. "Excuse me, ma'am. We're just gonna take Mr. Tough Guy here for a little ride in the cruiser." He reached for Jinx's arm.

"Hey!" Jinx yelled, attempting to pull away. "What'd *I* do? You can't arrest me!"

"You're right," the shorter cop said, "we can't, but—"

"*Why?*" Star blurted out. "Why can't you arrest him? Look what he did!"

"We have to witness it," the blond cop answered. He tightened his grip till Jinx's lip curled. "But we *can* have a nice man-to-man talk. Let's go, buddy. Outside. Vamoose."

Star and me watched as the headlights slipped backward down the dark driveway. Mama jerked the strings on the blinds. The white slats fell closed, like heavy lids dropping shut on three giant eyes. By the time she spun around, her tears had dried. Her face was red now, angry. "Which one of you called the police?"

Star and me stood side by side, nearly touching. Her mouth fell open, but no sound escaped.

Mama's eyes traveled back and forth between us. "Well?"

"I called them," Star said.

Mama stepped closer. "Star, how *could* you? Look at the shame you brought to this family!"

"Shame?" Star hollered back. "What's shame got to do with anything?"

"Guaranteed," Mama said, "everybody on this street is wagging their jaw right now about how the police arrived at the Thorn place. How Lyle Thorn was taken away in a cop car. How his wife can't keep peace enough to—"

"Mama!"

"People don't go airing their family problems like that, Star. It's humiliating!" She huffed past. "Every marriage has problems. Your pa and I had problems."

Star ducked into the bathroom and returned quickly, thrusting the hand mirror in front of Mama's face. "Did you ever look like *this* after you and Pa fought? Did you?"

Mama pushed Star's hand away and stomped toward the kitchen.

Star was on her heels. "I was scared, Mama! Can't you understand that? Can't you see what it's like for me and Blue?"

Mama ran water from the tap. She winced when the glass touched her lips.

"Look, Star. What went on was between Lyle and me. Period. It's not your concern."

"Not my concern?" Star squeezed in between Mama and the sink. "How do you figure that? Lyle Thorn is beating on our mama, the only parent me and my sister have left—hell, he could put her in the grave beside our pa, for all we know—and it's none of our blessed business? Go ahead, Mama, explain that one to me. I really would like to know!"

Mama looked away, sipping water. We never did get to hear her answer, if she even had one, 'cause footsteps sounded on the porch steps. The front door flew open, and the tall blond cop led Jinx inside. "Okay, Mr. Thorn, remember what we talked about."

Lyle slumped forward like a kid just back from the principal's office.

"No more BS," the shorter one added. "Buy yourself a punching bag if you want something to beat on."

They pulled the door closed behind them.

Lyle sulked toward Mama, apologizing a dozen times, at least.

"It's okay," she told him. "I was partly to blame. I didn't have to get so nasty about the ketchup."

Star's Frye boots hammered up the stairs. "Mama," she screamed, slamming our bedroom door closed, "you're just as sick as he is!"

A comment like that usually got Star grounded for a week, but not this time. Mama was too busy making up with Jinx. He asked her out for a drink, and she slipped into the bathroom, caked on more skin-colored cream, then followed him out the door without saying so much as good-bye.

Upstairs, Star leaned into her bureau mirror, brushing sky-blue shadow on her eyelids. So much had gone on I didn't stop to wonder why she was prettying herself up at that hour. I threw myself across my bed so hard the water in Little Ricky's bowl splashed back and forth. "They're going out for drinks," I said, raising my voice over the record album blaring on her turntable. "Lyle Ethan Thorn has been bailed out once more."

"*I'm* ready to get bailed out, too!" Star shouted back, reaching for her mascara. "Bailed out of this loony bin."

A strange and unfamiliar smile crossed her lips.

It never once occurred to me that Star wasn't kidding.

✲

Star fell asleep first. I counted the ceiling boards—thirty-six across, Mama's age—over and over till I heard the rumble of Jinx's truck.

I opened our bedroom door a crack and watched Mama and Jinx stumble up the steps, drunker than skunks, as Pa would've said. They stopped at the landing. Jinx leaned forward, kissing Mama hard.

She took a step back. "Ouch, sweetie, that hurts."

"Oh, Ceil," Jinx slurred, touching Mama's face. "I can't believe what I did to you. I don't *deserve* you. I love you way more than I should, I know that's my problem. I need you so much it makes me crazy." He fell to his knees, burying his face in Mama's skirt. "Oh, Lord, I'm sorry . . . I'm sorry. . . ."

Mama smoothed his hair. She helped him stand.

Their bedroom door groaned closed.

In the morning, Star was gone, her pale sheets twisted to the side. A purple envelope was propped on her pillow. I tore it open, my hands shaking.

> *Dear Blue,*
>   *Please don't be mad at me. I can't take another day in this place.*
>   *I'll be back for you soon, little sister. Promise!*
>   *Until then,*
>   *Star*

Mama cried when I showed her the note. She waited till Jinx left for work, then phoned the police. The officer with the blond sideburns took the report. Mama rounded up some photographs to give him. I blushed, describing the last thing I'd seen Star wearing—the old bleached-out T-shirt she slept in. It was one of Pa's, from Barry's Billiards, white with an eight ball on the front pocket and their motto over the top: WE'VE GOT ALL THE BALLS YOU'LL EVER NEED.

He slid Star's pictures into his pocket. "We'll do all we can."

I watched from the window while his car pulled out. I was having one of those déjà-vu experiences Star'd told me about—where your mind says, *I've seen this before.* 'Cause that's how it felt, watching those headlights inch down the driveway again.

Mama walked over to me. I wouldn't have recognized her by her silhouette, her face was so swollen. "Blue?" she started. It sounded like *Plue* on account of her fat lip.

I stared at the empty driveway, at the wide, black cracks, thinking how much they looked like rivers in the moonlight. "Yeah, Mama?"

"Blue, you . . . you think it's my fault Star left, don't you?" She pinched her eyes closed. Probably so she wouldn't have to see the truth spelled out all across my face.

I didn't answer, and Mama didn't ask again.

She pulled the blinds. The dark eyes blinked closed.

Déjà vu.

eight

It was almost six, and Mama hadn't called from Cape Cod yet.

I stood in front of the microwave while my TV dinner heated, watching the frozen yellow blob on the mashed potatoes melt.

Busy, busy, my mind was, without a second to rest. Star always accused me of thinking too much. *Freeing your mind is an important thing,* she'd tell me. I walked in on her once while she was doing just that, meditating. She sat twisted like a pretzel, burning smelly incense, *ummmm*-ing and *ohhhhhh*-ing like she'd stubbed all ten toes at once. That settled that: If my sister's mind was a wide open field, and mine was a busy playground, I'd take the creaky swings and rusty teeter-totters any day.

I'd set the table just how I wanted it. The music box from Pa sat beside my chocolate milk, and the photograph of Mama and Star and me leaned against the bowl of plastic fruit. I was imagining a *real* family dinner, the kind we used to have, but it was feeling more like one of those séances Star had told me about.

The microwave dinged. I picked kernel corn off the mashed potatoes and wound the music box. Again and again, the whole time I ate, never letting the last note chime. "Blue Bayou" played nine times in all. I was just about to grab the fudge brownie, which I always saved for last, when the phone rang. I figured it'd be Mama.

"Hello?" The line was quiet. "Hello?"

I eyed the brownie from across the kitchen. I tugged on the phone cord, trying to reach it. "Hel-*looo*-ooo?"

I heard music on the other end. Real faint. "Hey, who *is* this?"

I waited, listening. I recognized the song. It was the one Star and me danced to in the kitchen the night Pa won the money. "Take It to the Limit." The hairs on my arms prickled. "Star?" I asked. "Is that you?"

The music stopped. I thought my heart was going to stop right along with it. I licked my lips, but the pasty potato taste just made them stickier. I asked again, "Star, is that you?"

The person cleared her throat.

"*Star?*"

"Yes, Blue. Yes."

"Where are you?"

The line crackled. "Blue, don't say anything. Just listen. Okay?"

I was squeezing the phone so hard I could feel my pulse in my fingernails. I nodded, even though Star couldn't see.

"Are you alone?" she asked.

I nodded again.

"Is that a yes, Blue?"

"Yeah, sorry," I whispered. "I'm alone."

"Good. Great. Where is everyone?"

My voice was jigglier than Jell-O. "You said not to talk."

"Blue, you told me you're alone. Of *course* you can talk."

"Oh, yeah . . . sorry."

"Stop apologizing. Where is everyone?"

"Jinx drove Mama out to Cape Cod. Yar-something."

"Yarmouth? You don't have to whisper, Blue."

"Yeah, that's it. Yarmouth. Star, where *are* you?"

"What are they doing in Yarmouth? They never go away."

"I know, but this time they did. It's their anniversary."

"Big whoop."

"Yeah, big whoop all right. Star, tell me where you are."

"I can't just yet. But I'm fine."

"Come *on,* Star."

"Blue, I can't talk long. I just wanted to tell you that— well, I haven't forgotten the promise I made. I'm working on a plan. In the meantime, I'd like to see you. You're out of school now, right? How's lunch?"

"How's *lunch*? Star, how can you seriously ask me that? I've been talking to you in my head every second since you left." I forced a swallow. "I mean, how could you just leave me all alone here?"

"Blue, I told you in my note, I couldn't stand it any-more, okay?"

"And you think *I* can, Star? Part of how I hung on was 'cause of you. Jinx may be a mean old son of a so-and-so, but you hurt my feelings way more than he ever could. You're supposed to know better. You're supposed to—"

"Blue, I'm hanging up!"

"Don't! When can I see you?"

The operator cut in, telling Star to put in more money. I listened for the sound of a coin dropping.

Nothing.

"Star . . . ?"

"Soon. Give me some days that are good for you. Days Mama and Jinx both work. I don't want to bump into either of them. I'll check my schedule and get back to you—"

"Your *schedule*?"

"Yes, Blue. My schedule. I'm not on vacation here, I've got responsibilities."

"How about your responsibilities to us, Star? To *me*?"

"Blue, I said I'm working on it. Now, when are Romeo and Juliet coming back?"

"Tomorrow night."

"Good. I'll call before then. If you talk to Mama, don't tell her you heard from me. Promise?"

"Okay, but—" I was about to ask her why when we got cut off. I stood there for the longest time, clutching that dang phone, like something else was going to come leaping out of it. Like the dial tone droning on the side of my head had a life all its own.

"How's lunch?" I muttered.

&

Upstairs, I dragged the phone out of Mama and Jinx's room, parking it on the floor beside my bed.

I reached below my mattress for the black hardbound sketchbook Pa'd bought me for my tenth birthday. Paper-clipped to a drawing I'd started was a Polaroid our old neighbor'd taken of Mama and Pa and Star and me one Easter Sunday. Pa was wearing his navy-blue sports jacket. Mama had on her white peasant dress and big hoop earrings, a corsage Pa'd bought her pinned below one shoulder. Star and me were wearing dresses Mama'd made. Star's was yellow pinstripes, and mine was lavender flowers. My slip was showing from the long reach to loop my arm across Star's shoulder.

I liked using photographs to draw portraits. Most people can't sit still long enough for you to sketch them, but pictures let you take your sweet time.

Using colored pencils, I began coloring Star's hair, blending burnt sienna with yellow ochre.

The phone rang and I jumped, sending a gold line shooting through Star's dress. I reached toward the floor, grabbing the receiver. *"Star?"*

There was a long silence.

"Blue?" It was Mama. "Blue, why did you answer the phone that way?"

Heat crept across my face. "Um, what way?"

"You know very well what way. You answered the phone yelling your sister's name. Blue, did . . . did you hear from Star?"

I hated lying to Mama, but I had given Star my word. "No," I said. "I—I was just working on Star's portrait, that's all." I stared down at her copper-colored hair. I coughed, then threw in some sniffling noises. "I guess I felt so close to her, I just shouted out her name."

Must be Mama bought it, 'cause when she finally spoke, she changed the subject. "It's really nice here, Blue."

I let out the breath I'd been holding. "Yeah? How so?"

"Our room's pretty. Decorated in tans and blues. Beach paintings. Seashell lamps. You name it." A top popped and Mama took a long swig of something. Probably one of Jinx's Miller beers. "The balcony's small, it's really just a tiny deck. It's not big enough for both of us. Just Lyle and his beer cooler—he's out there now, as a matter of fact. Oh, and it looks out over the parking lot instead of the ocean, like it said in the ad, but"—Mama took another long sip—"it's still wonderful."

I glanced at the clock on my nightstand. Eight-thirty. I prayed Star wasn't trying to call.

"Let's see, what else? It's warm here. Downright tropical." She laughed. Took another sip. "The air conditioner doesn't work, but Lyle, he thought of everything. He brought the box fan."

I looked at the clock again. The hands hadn't moved.

"So," Mama said, "did you eat your TV dinner?"

"Yeah, I did. The fried chicken one. It was good. Thanks."

"What were you doing when I called?"

"Drawing. Remember?"

"Oh, right. Sorry."

I stared at Mama's face in the photograph. A wave of missing her jabbed at my insides. "I'm glad to hear your voice. I'm glad you're okay."

Must be Jinx came in off the deck 'cause I could hear him kissing her, making slurping noises. Mama started *tee-hee*-ing. These were the same sounds I'd heard coming from the porch the night I decided to eavesdrop on Star and her old boyfriend. The slurping sounds got closer still. I held the phone away from my ear, half expecting the little holes on the clunky black receiver to start oozing saliva.

Mama's voice drifted through the open space. "I'll let you get back to your drawing, Blue. We're going to go take a walk on the beach and watch the sun set."

I pictured the huge yellow ball of fire crash-landing behind Mama's hotel. I imagined her and Jinx walking straight toward it, into it. Disappearing. My words seized up in my throat. "Okay," I pinched out. "Bye."

"Blue?" Mama called. "Wait—"

I held the receiver close again. The slurping noises had stopped. "Yeah?"

Mama's voice was warm as a nightgown fresh out of the dryer. "I miss you, Baby Blue."

My eyes filled with tears. It took everything I had in me not to blink.

"Me too," I said, and hung up.

nine

It was morning before the phone rang again. It woke me out of a sound sleep. "Hello?"

"Blue?" It was Star. "Are you up?"

It was just getting light out. I squinted at the clock's glow-in-the-dark numbers. Five after five. "I am now," I said. "What happened? I thought you were calling back. I stayed up till after midnight waiting."

"Did Mama call? You didn't tell her we talked, did you?"

"No . . . I mean yes . . . I mean, wait a minute." I clicked on the light by my bed, like that was going to help me think clearer. "Yes, Mama called. No, I didn't let on we talked." I held the phone close. I could smell my breath bouncing back on me. "Star, where *are* you?"

I sat on the edge of the bed. Bud scratched his head against my elbow.

"I'm in the same state you're in. That's all I'm saying."

"Massachusetts?" I shouted, so loud I scared Bud off the bed. "You're in *Massachusetts*?"

"That'd be the one, Blue. Unless you moved and forgot to mention it."

"You're edgy, Star. Are you hungry?" That always made her nasty. It's that low blood sugar thing.

"Look, Blue. I can't talk long."

A muffled voice came over what sounded like an intercom. Star cupped her hand over the phone. I only caught parts of what it said. *Bradley Airport . . . Hartford . . . something, something. . . .*

"Blue? Are you still there?"

"What was that?"

"Nothing. Never mind. Where was I? Oh, right, I—" The operator cut in, telling Star to put in more money. "And whose turn might it be to interrupt me next?" she snapped.

"Star? You got any money?"

She took her time answering. "Yes."

"Put it in."

Thank God this was one of those few-and-far-between times Star actually did something somebody else's way. I listened as a single coin dropped.

"Listen, Blue. This doesn't mean I've got all day."

"Star, I miss you."

I waited for her to say something back.

"Star?"

She cleared her throat. Crumpled a paper.

I swallowed hard. "I think about you all the time. It's like I'm half a person since you left. Maybe a quarter of one. An eighth, even. I—"

Star broke in, probably figuring she ought to, before I divided myself up so small there'd be nothing left of me. "I miss you, too," she said. "I know you probably find that hard to believe, under the circumstances, but I miss you a lot."

I closed my eyes, letting the words swim around inside of me. "You do?"

"Of course I do. You're my sister. Leaving you wasn't something I *wanted* to do, it was something I *had* to do . . ."

". . . *Springfield to New York City, now loading at gate six, stopping in Hartford,*" a voice boomed. "*That's Peter Pan to New York, now loading . . .*"

It was hard not leaping out of my skin when I realized where Star was. At the bus terminal in Springfield, just a half hour away.

"Blue?"

"Yeah?"

"What do you think?"

I knew I'd missed something she said, but the answer had to be yes since 99 percent of Star's questions had to do with getting somebody to agree with her. "Yeah," I said. "I know what you mean."

The operator came on again. I waited for the sound of more coins.

"Star?"

A second coin clinked.

I had to think fast. I needed to find a way to keep Star where she was, to make sure she didn't hop on one of those buses and disappear for another whole month.

It came to me, all at once. *"Oooooow,"* I moaned, holding my stomach, praying I could pull off the humdinger I was about to tell.

"Blue, what's the matter?"

"My stomach hurts."

"What's wrong with your stomach?"

"Well, actually, it's not my stomach. It's lower. I have these strange aches I've never had before. They're like—"

"Cramps?" I could hear the excitement in her voice.

"Maybe . . ."

I tried to remember everything I could about Star's first period. How she woke one morning with a small stain in her underpants. Mama took her into the bathroom and showed her the contents of the old blue Avon suitcase she kept her feminine products in. After that the door closed and what went on behind it was a mystery to me. When it opened again, my sister was a different person. Everything about her seemed older.

Star sounded worried. "Blue, are you okay?"

"I think so, but—*ooooooow!*—can you call me back?"

"Why?"

"I have to go to the bathroom." I lowered my voice for special effect. "I feel something going on down there. Hang on, I'm gonna look." I held the phone near my belly as I snapped the elastic on my pajama bottoms. "Star! Oh, my God, I'm bleeding!"

"Blue, relax, please. You've just got"—she paused, then whispered the rest—"your period."

"Oh . . ."

"Blue, I can't believe this is happening when there's no one there to help you. Damn. Why'd Mama have to pick this weekend to go out of town?"

"It's okay, Star. You'll talk me through it, won't you?"

"Of course I will, Blue."

"Good. I'm going to look for the Avon suitcase. Call me back in five minutes?"

"Sure, Blue, I'll—"

Star didn't have a chance to finish 'cause we got cut off. That was okay, though. The line may have been dead, but my plan was fully alive.

ten

I dug through the junk drawer Jinx kept his matches in, searching till I found the one with the number on it I was looking for.

I dialed the phone. A woman answered. "Yes? Hello?" I could tell I was waking her up.

I made my voice go deep. "Is this Pioneer Taxi?" I should've practiced first. I sounded like a walrus.

"Just a minute," she answered. "Stewart? . . . Stewart? . . . Wake up, Stew, it's for you."

"Yeah, this is Stewart." His voice was scratchy. "Pioneer Taxi. Whatever."

I got an instant picture of Stewart in my mind. Like my brain had snapped a Polaroid of him sitting on the edge of his bed with his tired face and his messed-up night hair and his full belly flopping over a pair of funny-looking boxer shorts.

I tried my deep voice again. "Stewart, I need a taxi." Much better.

I heard him light a cigarette. "Do you know what time it is?"

"Hang on." I checked the clock. "It's five-thirty."

Stewart laughed till he coughed. "Well, I guess you *do* know. Where you going?"

"Springfield. The bus station."

"What time you need to be there?"

"Soon. *Real* soon." I gave him our address. I could hear him rustling around.

"Okay," he said. "I'll be there in a half hour."

"Um, how about fifteen minutes?"

Stewart laughed again. "Okay. You got it."

✍

I threw on a T-shirt and shorts and downed a bottle of cola. Bud got a can of Flaked Salmon Supreme for breakfast, and I got zilch.

Star called back seven minutes later. "Sorry," she said, out of breath. "Someone was using the phone. How are you doing? Did you find the suitcase? Did you figure everything out?"

"Yeah, I did." I threw in a heavy sigh. "But these *cramps*—"

"I know, they're the worst."

"Isn't there something I can do?"

"There should be some Midol in the medicine cabinet. Take some and lay down with a hot water bottle. Oh, Blue, I feel so bad about not being there to help you. . . ."

"I wish you were here too. But, well, there is *something* you could do. . . ."

"Name it."

"How long does the Midol take to work?"

"I don't know. A half hour maybe. Why?"

"Can you call me back in a half hour and see how I'm feeling? Unless you want to give me the number there."

"That's okay. I'm at a pay phone. I'll hang out and call back."

"Thanks, Star. I feel better knowing you'll check on me."

"Sure, little sister. I'll talk to you soon."

A car horn tooted.

Bud yowled, looking to go out. "I told you, I don't have time." I opened the downstairs closet door, pointing at the litter box inside. "Fair's fair. I missed my breakfast so you could have yours. The least you can do is poop indoors."

Again, the horn blew. On my way out I grabbed a stick of Jinx's peppermint gum to make up for not brushing my teeth.

The passenger-side door was pushed open. I walked the long way around the tall grass.

"You're a *kid*," Stewart said.

"I'm thirteen," I lied, sliding in, snapping my seat belt. "Can we go?"

"You got the moola for this?" He looked just like the picture I had of him in my mind. All except for the curly hairs sprouting out his ears. Those I'd missed.

I waved a hundred dollars in twenties in front of him.

Don't worry, Pa. It's just a loan. It's for a real good cause. You'll see.

"Guess you do," Stewart said. He put the car in drive, tipping his head to look at Jinx's house before we drove off. "If you don't mind my saying, you guys ought to spend some of your money on a new roof."

I knew right then I had an ally. "I agree," I said, "but it's not my house."

Stewart looked confused.

"Baby-sitting. I just work there." I looked back. "I say there could be a giant tick party going on in that front yard and they'd never know it."

Stewart laughed. "No doubt on that one."

I had the color of his teeth pegged right, too. Dingy yellow. Maybe Star wasn't the only one who was psychic in this family.

Stewart veered onto the I-91 ramp. The pale hills

stretched out on both sides of us. "What's your name?" he asked.

"Blue."

"Seriously?" Stewart squinted so hard his fat bristly eyebrows touched, melting into one big long one. "Blue like the color blue?"

I nodded.

Stewart smiled, clicking on the radio. It was set on the classical station. The Constipated Station, as Jinx called it. Violin notes sprang out of the dashboard, shoving into each other like they were in a mad rush to get somewhere. It made me jittery.

Stewart bounced his head to the rhythm, if that's what you'd call it. "That's easy enough to remember," he said, and I realized he was still thinking about my name. "Yeah . . . Blue. Blue with a lotta green dough."

&

Stewart wove in and out through the viaducts, tunnels wrapping over our heads like huge concrete snakes. The gray sky slid sideways past the giant letters: B-U-S. Stewart pulled behind another cab.

"How much do I owe you?" I asked.

Stewart snuffed out a cigarette. "Fifteen'll do it."

The money was soggy from my hand sweat. I handed

him a twenty. "Keep the change," I told him, remembering how Pa'd said good tipping was a class act.

"Want me to wait here?" he said. "Make sure—?" He waved his hand.

"It's okay," I said. "But thanks."

Stewart pulled away.

My heart raced. I don't know what scared me more. Not finding Star or finding her. But one thing I did know for sure. I had to pee something awful.

I passed through the giant doors. My sneakers squeaked on the speckled tile. Music seeped from the walls. They were playing Stewart's station. Horns were tooting, and cymbals were crashing, and I was almost wishing they'd bring back the violins.

I passed by the pay phones.

The snack bar.

No sign of Star.

By now I had to pee so bad I was saying prayers I'd make it. I passed a man loading luggage. "Excuse me. Which way to the bathrooms?"

He pointed with his chin toward the double doors. "Straight through. On the right."

It was pretty dang hard trying to walk and squeeze my legs together at the same time. I thought of Stewart. "That's easy. Blue with the green dough and the yellow puddle."

The first stall I tried didn't lock. I ducked into the second and dropped my shorts just in time, peeing out all twelve ounces of cola and then some. I retied my sneakers, waiting for the last burst to stop. I noticed the person in the next stall had Frye boots like Star's, except not as dark.

The wall between us rattled as her door bolted open. I pulled my shorts up and flushed, watching through the crack while she walked to the sink.

She was tall. Her red hair was cut close to her head. She bent forward, splashing water on her face.

I pushed my door open and walked toward her, studying the scar on her arm. It was nearly three inches long, shaped like the state of Florida.

Water dripped off her pointy chin while she reached for a paper towel.

My chest rose and fell and rose and fell. I couldn't catch my breath.

She dabbed at her face. Her reflection floated back to the glass. Our eyes met in the mirror.

"Hell's bells," she mumbled.

"Hi, Star. . . ."

Star stared at me, her mouth dropped open. "Blue, I've been trying to call you. I thought you were—I mean, how did—"

"Star . . ." I was so nervous I'd ripped a hangnail open

and was squeezing two fingers together trying to keep the blood off my shirt. "I have a confession to make. I didn't really get my period. I lied to you." My hands shook. My hangnail oozed blood. "I'm sorry. But I needed to see you. Now."

Star raked her watermelon-colored nails through her short hair. "I told you to wait. I told you I was working on something."

"But you're glad to see me, aren't you?" I took a step toward her. "You're not mad at me, are you?"

I didn't wait for her answer. A spring inside me popped loose, sending me soaring right into Star's arms, which, thankfully, she opened just in time.

I hugged Star as hard as my arms would let me with all the shaking they were doing. I could feel her heart going *ka-thump, ka-thump* on my shoulder, could feel her crisp hair ends crush themselves against my cheek. I breathed in the incense smell on her gauze shirt. The breath went deep. Clear down to my toes.

Star let go first. She took a step back, grinning at me.

"What, Star? What is it?"

Star ducked down low. It took me a second to realize she was checking for feet beneath the stalls. "It won't be long," she said, draping her arm across my shoulder. I got my first good look at her burn scar.

"Huh?"

"Before you *really* get your period."

"Yeah? How do you know that?"

Star pushed a strand of hair behind my ear. Her eyes dropped down to the tiny bumps on my chest. "Once *they* start growing, it's just a matter of time. Weeks. Maybe days."

"That's good to know," I said. "Thanks."

"Hey, what are big sisters for?"

I was just about to tell her how much I'd missed her—and how glad I was to be there with her in the ladies' bathroom of the Springfield bus station discussing puberty like she'd only been gone five minutes—when she leaned close, picking a Bud hair off my T-shirt. "Hey, Blue?"

"Yeah?"

I thought she was going to let me in on another divine secret of womanhood—Star with her very own period and her breasts full-grown, from the looks of things—but she didn't.

Her whisper tickled my ear. "You got any money on you? I'm *starved*."

eleven

I sat across from Star at the Sunny Side Up Restaurant, staring at the English muffin I'd ordered.

"How come you're not eating?" Star asked, shaking ketchup on her hash browns. She'd ordered the Three Egg Breakfast Bonanza. Star took after Pa. She could eat anything in sight and still stay skinny as a number-two pencil.

"I'm not hungry," I said. The truth is, I was starving. But the fat black fly making his way across the buttery, crisp top of my muffin was killing off my appetite. I couldn't help thinking how he used to be a maggot. That he could be making our table his next stop after traipsing across a fresh pile of dog doo. I pushed the plate away. "So . . . when'd you start drinking coffee?"

Star ripped the corner off her fourth sugar and stirred it in. She looked like Pa with her hair cut short. "The woman I've been staying with drinks it," she said. "I used to think it tasted like sludge, but now I love it. Try a sip?"

"No thanks. This woman you've been staying with, what's her name?"

"Sherry. Sherry Pinsky. She's a vegetarian, like Mama." Star sipped her coffee, made a face, and tore open another sugar. "We eat tofu all the time."

I made a face, recalling the time Mama made us try it, all slimy and damp like a chunk of wet sponge, and nothing much to report on as far as taste was concerned. "You mean you *eat it* eat it? As in chew-it-up-and-swallow-it eat it?"

Star shook pepper on her eggs. "Definitely. Sherry's got tofu recipes you wouldn't believe."

I leaned forward, smashing dried-up toast crumbs into my elbows. "Where'd you meet her?"

"Hmmm?"

"Sherry." I was already set not to like her. "Where'd you two find each other?"

"When I first left I hitchhiked to this shelter for battered women. Most of the women had kids with them." She mashed a piece of rye toast into her egg yolk and downed it.

I waited, tapping my fingers on the underside of the table. I felt a wad of gum there and pulled my arm back, knocking my funny bone good on the back of our booth.

Star swallowed. "I lied. I said I was eighteen. Had a boyfriend who hit me. Blah, blah, blah. I pretty much used Mama's story, since *she'll* never get around to telling it to anybody."

"Star, you don't know that for sure."

"Well, that remains to be seen." Star popped a sausage in her mouth and washed it down with tomato juice. "I was there two or three days when Sherry came in with her son, Randall, who, as it turns out, sleepwalks. Sherry'd wake up looking for him, and half the time I'd be up already, so I'd help her track him down." Star laughed. "Once we found him in the kitchen, peeing in the bread drawer. Standing there with this trancy look in his eyes and that little thing of his hanging out, wetting down six loaves of white bread." Star looked up, probably expecting I'd be laughing, too.

I wasn't. This Sherry person was getting on my nerves.

"Anyway, Sherry used to live with this guy. And if he doesn't sound like he could be Jinx's twin. Sherry's even got a partial from him."

"A partial? A partial *what?*"

"You know," she said. "A *partial*." Like saying it again was going to make me understand. Star rolled her eyes. "Blue, a partial's a row of fake teeth a dentist makes for you when your real ones come out. In Sherry's case, they got knocked out. Four of them."

I ran my tongue across the front of my teeth. They

were fuzzy-feeling from not getting brushed. "So, where's this shelter you're staying at?"

"Stayed," she said. "Past tense. We're not there anymore." She plucked the last bite of hash browns off her plate before the waitress whisked by, snatching it away. "It was in Greenfield, where Sherry's from. It's not some place you'd recognize from the street, though. It just looks like a plain old—"

"Greenfield? You were that close and you didn't call me?"

"Blue, you can't make phone calls from a shelter. It's a secret place. And you can't have company there, either, if you're wondering why I didn't invite you over for Sunday dinner."

I hated when Star got sarcastic. I sat back, folding my arms.

Star stretched her legs into the aisle. "Look, Blue . . . I'm *sorry*, okay?"

Fighting tears, I stared at the toes of her boots. They were gray and dull and scratched. They needed one of Pa's good polishings.

"We moved into an apartment last week," Star continued. "Here in Springfield. No phone still. That's why I called you from the bus station. They open early. I never could sleep late. You know me. . . ."

Yeah, I *thought* I knew her.

The waitress flew past, refilling Star's coffee. I watched her start with the sugars again.

"I baby-sit Randall in exchange for rent. Sherry has a degree in cosmetology. She's assistant manager at the New You Hair Salon." Star stirred her coffee. "Ever hear of it?"

"Sorry."

Star shrugged her shoulders. "Sherry's getting promoted to manager soon. Then, in the fall, when Randall's in kindergarten, she's going to hire me to work there, too. I'll start small—sweeping and shampooing—but I'll work my way up soon enough."

I couldn't believe my ears. My sister, the beautiful and talented Star Hanson, was going to settle for scrubbing scalps and bagging split ends. "Star, what about marching band and swim practice? And summer theater? They practically promised you the lead part!"

It was like Star didn't hear me. "Sherry says I've got natural-born haircutter's hands."

"You can't just stay out of school. That's illegal."

"Well," Star snapped, "too bad beating on your wife isn't."

"Beating on your wife isn't *legal,* Star. They just need to catch him in the act."

The fly was back, crawling across a tiny triangle of toast the waitress had missed. I stared at my lap, working up the nerve to ask what I'd been wanting to. "How long are you planning on staying here?"

"Blue"—Star leaned forward—"I *live* here now. And as soon as Sherry gets her raise for becoming manager, I'm going to ask her if you can come live with us, too." She studied my face. "Don't you get it? This is *the Plan*. This is what I've been working on all this time."

No, I guess I didn't get it. I tried picturing life without Mama, and—Jinx or no Jinx—I just couldn't. I looked away. "So, why'd you call?"

"What, a person can't call her own sister?" Star looked away, folding her napkin into a little white cube.

"Star, there's something you're not telling me."

She flattened the paper cube with her thumb. "I saw something in my cards, that's all."

"Who sends you cards?" I asked.

"Blue, don't be dense. I'm talking about *tarot* cards. You know, as in tell-the-future?"

"I remember," I said. "What's the big deal?"

Star's face was pale.

I touched her hand. "Star, *what*?"

Star slid her hand out from under mine. She reached in the pouch she wore at her side and pulled out the deck of cards she was talking about. "Every card has a special meaning," she said, fanning them out on the table between us.

"Yeah. So?"

Star sucked in her bottom lip, biting on it. "The same card keeps showing up. Every time I ask a question about Mama."

"Really? Which one?"

Star's fingers swept across the arc of cards. Her long melon-colored nails nudged one loose. She slid it forward, toward me.

I studied the picture. A skeleton was riding a horse, carrying a black flag.

"I don't get it."

Star's fingers backed off the card, exposing the word they'd been covering. Chills rippled through me. I was about to say the word out loud when Star beat me to it. "It's the death card, Blue."

Star explained about the death card. How it doesn't always mean *death* death, as in somebody up and dying. It could be symbolic, meaning maybe the person's going to lose a job or have a car conk out.

"But you're not thinking it's symbolic, are you Star? You're worried it means—" I couldn't say it.

Star collected the cards, clutching them tight. "I'm fearful for Mama, Blue. Why can't she be more like Sherry? Sherry saw the light. She got out *before* it was too late." She tucked the cards into her pouch, avoiding my eyes. "Blue, I'd love nothing more than for you to tell me I'm wrong. That this death card business sounds crazy to you. That Mama and Jinx are off on some dumb romantic vacation getting along just peachy now that I'm not there butting my nose in every two seconds. Tell me, Blue. Tell me I've been dreaming this all up."

Star was looking to the wrong person for reassurance. I had enough worries of my own about Mama without hauling the death card into it.

"What do you think?" Star asked.

I squinted my eyes, trying to focus. My mind flipped in circles like the ring of index cards Pa'd kept his trucking numbers on. Every flip flashed an image.

Jinx's raised fist. *Flip.*

Mama's bleeding mouth. *Flip. Flip.*

Mama in the truck next to Jinx, backing away. Mama's kiss pressed on the window screen. *Flip. Flip. Flip.*

"Blue?" Star squeezed my arm. "Earth to Blue?"

My teeth chattered.

"Blue, are you okay?"

Our waitress was next to me now, leaning in close. Her perfume smelled like bug spray. Her mouth moved in red elastic circles. I stared at the lipstick smudge on her teeth. My head prickled, like it was getting filled in with sand. Something was eating up all the light spaces.

Star? What's going on?

Everything went black.

§

I smelled something. Ammonia. My nose hairs burned.

The floor was cold on my back. I opened my eyes, staring up at the underside of a small round table. A fan twirled on the ceiling.

"Blue?" Star asked. "Are you all right?" She was kneeling beside me, patting my hand like Florence Nightingale, while our waitress waved a white stub under my nose.

When I realized that's what smelled, I pushed her hand away. "Hey, what are you trying to do to me with that thing?"

"She's conscious!" she yelled, and that time I heard her. But then, I'm sure the whole entire city of Springfield did, too. "Praise the Lord!"

I tapped Star's knee. "How'd I get here?"

Star shuddered. "You keeled over, Blue. Passed out cold."

Patches of light wavered in front of me. I leaned on Star to sit up.

The waitress looked on, smiling, like she'd just witnessed a religious miracle. She laid a bony hand on my shoulder. I stared at the shiny crucifix dangling from her neck. Jesus's thorny crown was lined with fake diamonds. "Praise the Lord!" she yelled again, so loud she nearly knocked me back over.

It was Star's idea, escorting me back home. She was probably worried I'd get woozy again and slip off the bridge walking from where the bus left me. I pictured her drinking coffee with five sugars in Sherry's kitchen the next morning, the headlines of the *Union-News* reaching up to grab her by the throat: "Daughter Reunites with Dead Father in River Tragedy."

The next bus out was at 10:15.

Star and me waited at the station eating Necco Wafers from the vending machine. It was an unspoken rule that all the white, black, and purple ones were hers. "Sure this'll be okay with Sherry?" I asked her. Really, I didn't give a rat's rear end about Sherry. I was hoping Star'd take the opportunity to tell me how my safety was the single most important thing in the world to her. Instead she told me it was Sherry's day off and, besides, she thought she left her rune stones in the sock drawer.

A voice boomed over the intercom, announcing our bus.

"Come on," Star said. "Gate two."

The driver took our tickets. The bus vibrated like Pa's eighteen-wheeler.

Pa, let it go right with Star. Help me find a way to keep her and Mama and me together.

Star picked a seat near the back. I slid in next to her.

"Welcome to Peter Pan," our driver announced. I watched his face in the mirror, his dark curls shaking when the bus shook. "Our final destination will be U-Mass, making stops in Holyoke, Northampton, and Amherst."

Star pushed a lever and her seat tipped back. "Blue, you're absolutely positive Mama and Jinx aren't coming back till late tonight?" She checked her watch again. It had little zodiac symbols for numbers. The picture in the middle informed whoever cared to know that the moon was in Aries.

"That's what Mama said. Not till way past suppertime."

Star closed her eyes and kept them closed. Maybe she was meditating.

I stared out the window. The clouds were squished together like cotton balls. I couldn't figure the loneliness I was feeling, the strange yearning sizzling a hole through my heart.

Cars glided by on both sides of us. One like Mama's old Nova was stopped on the shoulder, its hazard lights blinking. It had New Jersey plates. BBN-469.

BBN. It only took me a second. "Baby Blue Needs a good cry."

Star opened her eyes halfway. "You talking to me?"

I shook my head.

"Who, then?"

My face ached from holding back tears. "Just myself," I answered. "Just myself."

twelve

Stewart gave us a ride from the Northampton bus station. He insisted on splitting one of his sardine and mustard sandwiches with me after Star got wound up and told him about me passing out from hunger.

"It was good seeing you again, Blue," he said, pulling into Jinx's driveway. Harp sounds flooded the cab. "And nice meeting your sister, too—whoops! Where'd she go?"

Star hopped out before Stewart came to a full stop and—not wanting to be seen by Madame Busybody next door—shot straight up the back steps, then squatted behind the long vinyl seat Jinx had salvaged from his last truck for porch furniture.

"Good seeing you, too," I said, inching the door closed, trying not to disturb the calm feeling the music gave me.

The toes of Star's boots poked out between the porch rails, her nails digging a row of half-moons in the maroon seat while she steadied herself. "Blue, *hurry!*"

"I'm coming, I'm coming. . . ."

"Hey, Blue." Stewart stuck his head out the window. "Take one of my business cards."

Star moaned as I turned back. One of her feet was caught in the porch rails. She fell backward minus one boot, which hung there, wedged midair between two posts.

"Thanks," I called, waving to Stewart as he backed out.

Star was quite a sight, trying to tiptoe and limp at the same time. "It took you long enough," she grumbled.

I worked her boot loose and brought it in.

Star was already in the kitchen, throwing open and slamming closed the cupboard doors like she used to get in trouble for. One final slam and she found what she was after. She ripped the seal on Jinx's off-limits Beer Nuts and poured herself a huge handful. "Blue, you're absolutely positive Mama and Jinx aren't coming back till tonight?"

"I've told you ten zillion times already. *Yes,* I'm sure."

Bud lumbered toward me. I bent to pet him.

"Oh, *please.*" Star balanced a nut between two long nails. "Don't tell me you're friends with Jinx's cats now?"

Crunch. The nut was history.

"Just Bud," I said, feeling the purr in his neck rattle. "Miller's dead."

"What happened?"

I straightened up, twirling the handle on the blinds over the sink to let the light in. "He got run over. Out front. Jinx found him, still warm and all."

"Wow. Was he pissed?"

"No. More sad than anything."

Star picked at a nut that was stuck in her teeth. "How touching."

It bothered me, knowing Star was looking down her nose at me for being nice to Bud. I had to settle the score. "Come on, Star. I can't see snubbing Bud just 'cause Jinx is a jerk. That's not the cat's fault." I stared down at my hands. I still had shovel blisters from burying his brother. "Besides . . ."

"Besides what?"

"Well, I kind of feel this *connection* to Bud. 'Cause of Miller being taken away from him and all."

"Blue, get a grip. Bud's a cat."

"No kidding, Star. Animals have feelings, too." I swallowed hard and turned my back on her, pretending I was watching something out the window. "I can't believe I've got to remind *you* of that. You, who wouldn't go fishing with Pa unless he poked the worm on the hook for you. You, Miss Blubberhead of the World when Pa sprayed the hornets' nests. Or have you outgrown that now that you've got a *schedule,* now that you've got *responsibilities?*"

Star stomped over, standing so close I could smell her nutty breath. I think she was fixing to throttle me, but her mind could have very well been changed when she saw the tears filling my eyes. She rested a hand on my back. "Oh, Blue . . ."

I rubbed my nose on the shoulder of my T-shirt. "See, I figure Bud misses Miller, well, you know"—I looked up, searching her eyes for some sign she was catching on—"misses him the same way I've missed you."

Star's hand fell away. "Blue, I had to leave. I was dying inside." She grabbed the nuts and shoveled another large handful in her mouth.

"And you think *I'm* not?"

"I told you, Blue. I have a plan."

Star walked toward the stairs. She turned before starting up. "I'm going to get my rune stones. When I come back, I suggest we change the topic of conversation."

I followed her as far as the bottom step. I squeezed the handrail, staring up at the hollow between her shoulder blades. "You want to know what *I* think, Star?"

Star stopped. She turned to face me. "I've got a hunch I'm going to hear it whether I want to or not, so why don't you just go ahead."

I stepped toward her, never letting my eyes drop. "I don't—I don't think—" My heart thundered in my ears.

"Yeeessss?"

"I—I don't think those rune stones of yours are going to tell you anything you don't already know."

She glared at me.

"And the same goes for those tarot cards. We both know Mama's been living under the shadow of that death card ever since she married Jinx." I clutched the railing and took another step. "I don't think any of this—this spirit stuff you throw yourself into is going to make one bit of difference. When it comes right down to it, it doesn't matter if the moon's in Jupiter or Aries or floating in the middle of the dang bathtub, for crying out loud, 'cause Mama's *still* married to Jinx. And I'm *still* stuck here watching him beat on her while you're off sipping coffee with this Sherry person, looking after her stupid sleepwalking kid instead of your own flesh-and-blood sister—" My voice broke.

Star folded her arms across her chest. "Blue, listen—"

"No, *you* listen!"

I took another step up. I was even with her now. "Star, I know why you left." I looked over my shoulder at the doorway she'd stretched herself across, trying to protect Mama. "But the part about Mama getting beat on—that's just half the reason. You also left 'cause Mama *betrayed* you. She sided with Jinx, a sicko wife-beater, over you. Over *us,* her own daughters. But you went and did the same thing, Star—picking Sherry and Randall over Mama and me—so don't stand there telling *me* how it feels when you're dying inside."

I stared at the skinny rows of dirt ground into the see-through plastic stair treads, waiting for Star to say something. She didn't. She was sniffling. I'd made her cry, and—I have to admit—I wasn't sorry I had.

Finally, I started back down.

Star followed me.

We sat at the kitchen table, across from each other. In the same spots we sat for dinner up till a month ago. The shadows on the table looked like prison bars again. This time it was Star being caged. Star, who thought leaving made her free. That life would be all hunky-dory shampooing heads and sweeping floors while Mama got slapped around—far enough away so she wouldn't have to hear the screams.

That's when I knew for sure—I couldn't leave Mama. And Star couldn't make me, any more than I could make her stay.

I touched her arm. "Hey, Star?"

She looked up. Her cheeks were damp from crying. Her hair had curled up on the sides, like it did when it got wet. "What?"

"Do you still have that dark crinkly skirt with the blotchy white designs all over it?"

Star smiled. It was like seeing a sun shower. "The one you said looks like open mouths?"

"Open mouths and rotten teeth. That's the one."

"I still have it. Why?"

"Remember how you told me it was abstract? That whatever I saw in that design said diddly-squat about the skirt and plenty about me?"

Star reached across the plastic grapes for a napkin and blew her nose. "Yeah."

"You were right."

Star loved being right. "How's that?"

"'Cause those big old hollering mouths on your skirt do *indeed* say something about me. That's what living here in Jinx's house has been like, like trying not to drown in a big black sea of screaming mouths."

part three

thirteen

I called Stewart for Star's ride back to Springfield.

She thundered down the stairs, carrying a backpack she'd left behind. "Randall threw up on my other one," she informed me. Like I cared. She took a teensy bottle from a side pocket and shook a few drops of brownish liquid into her hand, then rubbed it on her neck.

"That smells nice," I said.

"Thanks. Lavender oil. It calms anxiety." She hoisted the backpack over her shoulder. "Want some?"

"That's okay," I said. "I'm feeling pretty calm right now."

Star stood at the window, watching for signs of Stewart.

"You don't have to do that," I said.

"Hmmm?" Her breath was steaming the glass.

"You don't have to keep checking. He'll toot."

Star wrote her name in the window fog. "That's okay," she said. "I don't mind."

I had the curlicue stitch pattern on the back of her gauze shirt memorized. "I want you to leave me Sherry's phone number."

"I can't do that."

"Why not? What if something happens?"

"Blue, you need some B vitamins to boost your memory. I already told you, Sherry doesn't have a phone. You think I called from the bus station because I like the ambience?" She underlined her name. Just like Mama'd done on Jinx's card: *Lyle, underline, underline, underline.* Underlining makes somebody important. It makes them count in a big way.

"I'll call you again," she said. "Try to be the one to answer the phone. If I get Jinx or Mama, I'm hanging up."

"But, Star, Mama misses you, too."

She checked her watch. "Yeah, right."

"She does." I reached for her hand. Her fingers dangled in my palm like icicles. I let go.

Star stepped back from the window. "Hey, Blue?"

"Yeah?"

"Quick, look—"

Someone was turning in the driveway.

Star crouched below the window frame. "Blue, who is it?"

The car pulled clear to the end, stopping in front of

the broken-down garage. I squinted through the R of Star's name. It wasn't Stewart's cab. It was a tan station wagon.

"Well?"

"I'm pretty sure it's Beau Silver. . . . Yeah, it's him."

"What's *he* doing here?"

"How should I know? Checking on me, probably. Mama told him I was here alone and—wait! He's got somebody with him!"

Star yanked the bottom of my T-shirt. "Is it Aggie? See if it's Aggie."

I studied the shadow. "I don't think so. The hair's not big enough."

The door on Beau's side groaned open. He leaned on the horn getting out. Star jumped, smacking her head on the sill.

I stared down at her crooked part. "That was just the horn."

"Gee, Blue, thanks so much for telling me something I didn't already know."

The shadow in the passenger seat wasn't moving. Beau walked around and held the door open.

Star grabbed my arm before I could see who got out. "Blue, hide me! You've got to hide me!"

I motioned toward the coat closet underneath the stairs. "In there. Hurry!"

Star crawled over on her hands and knees. I pushed the door closed behind her.

"Blue, what *stinks* in here? I think— Oh, God, what'd I step in?"

"It's Bud's litter box. I forgot to change it. Now, be quiet. They're on the porch."

"They *who*?" The whites of Star's eyes flashed behind the wooden slats. "Blue, who's *with* him?"

"I didn't get to see. Shhhh!"

Beau's feet were heavy on the steps. The plank floorboards shook. I'd forgotten to pull up the door shade. I watched the two silhouettes shift around. I waited for Beau to knock.

He didn't.

"Blue?"

I swallowed hard. "Not now!"

A key turned in the lock.

✦

"I can't imagine where she'd be. It's not like Blue to wander off like that." The voice was Mama's.

I pressed my back to the wall near the coat closet.

"Blue?" Mama called. I could hear her piling stuff on the kitchen table. *"Blue?"*

I watched Star's eyes behind the door slats. Flecks of white and green. Nervous, darting. I hoped, for her sake, that the lavender oil was working.

"Blue, are you here?"

I took a deep breath. I stepped around the corner. Mama's Yarmouth stuff filled the table. Her back was to me. "I'm here, Mama. How come you're back so—" She turned to face me. My hands went limp at my sides. "No, Mama! *No!*"

Beau's eyebrows tipped in while he stared at the floor. He rubbed his chin, and the tail on his mermaid tattoo swished back and forth.

My eyes traveled back to Mama's face. To the red swell of her cheek. The puffy curve of her neck, the bruises lined up like a row of violet marbles.

"Come give me a hug," she said, holding her arms out. Her breath was starchy-smelling, like boiled potatoes.

She waited.

My body locked in place. I felt sick.

Mama's eyes widened. *"Blue . . . ?"*

My feet were heavy as the cinder blocks Pa used to put in the trunk of Mama's car to weigh it down for winter. I dragged them toward her. I looped my arms around her skinny waist. Her hot cheek rested on my hair. The words I'd hungered for lashed at me. "I missed you, Baby Blue."

I winced against their pain as Mama held tight, my face squished in the hollow below her jaw.

I studied Beau with my one free eye.

"Blue," he said, "your mama's been trying to call you from our place."

I pulled away, extra slow, so Mama wouldn't feel me leaving all at once. "I went for a walk," I lied.

Mama reached in the fridge for a cola. "Must have been some walk," she said, starting for the living room. Beau followed her. The little ceramic animals Mama'd collected out of the Red Rose Tea boxes clattered on the windowsill. I had my eye on the lion. He was near the edge.

Mama and Beau sat on the couch. They left a space in the middle for me. I ignored it and crossed the room, leaning on the arm of Jinx's recliner. I could see Star's eyes from there, could feel them on me, singeing my skin.

"So. . . ." I felt a loose thread on the chair arm, curling it round and round my finger. "What happened?"

"Beau picked me up in Cape Cod this morning. Early." Mama reached to pat Beau's shoulder. "Lyle— took off during the night."

I couldn't believe my ears. "He *left* you there?"

Mama nodded. "We'd stopped out for a drink after our walk on the beach. The bar was in a basement. They had the most beautiful flowering plants hanging in front of these little slim windows. They hardly got any light, but they had giant red blossoms. I couldn't take my eyes off of them. I kept wondering how something that pretty could flower in such darkness. When Lyle got up to use the bathroom, I asked the bartender what they were called. I thought if those plants could bloom there, then maybe they could survive in our backyard, too. The bartender didn't remember their name, but he took a business card from his pocket and, on the back, he wrote the address of the nursery where they'd bought them." Mama sipped her cola. "Lyle came back just as I tucked the card in my handbag. He . . . jumped to conclusions. He dumped my purse open on the bar. Everything fell out. My lipstick, my wallet, my"—Mama blushed—"personal stuff. I felt like I was in high school getting my locker searched. I was so embarrassed.

"Lyle found the business card. He ripped it to shreds, then dropped the pieces in the bartender's coffee cup. He stormed up the stairs. I followed him, trying to explain. He wouldn't let me. He accused me of terrible things. When we got back to the motel, I ran ahead to the office to see if they had another room available." Mama drew lines in the sweat on her cola bottle. "I had no idea how I was going to pay for a room of my own, but I thought that maybe if Lyle had some time to himself, he might come to his senses."

Mama reached for a tissue on the end table. "Lyle followed me inside. He wouldn't let me get another room. He grabbed me. I started crying. I said to the man behind the front desk, 'Please, do something. Make him stop.' The man put his hands up." Mama raised her arms in the air, like a TV holdup. "Then he shook his head and walked away. Lyle took ahold of my hair. He pulled me toward our room. I called for help. Doors opened a crack as we passed by, then closed."

Mama was rocking herself.

The clock over the TV ticked. A fly buzzed against the window screen.

"I should go," Beau said, checking his watch. "I gotta get back to work."

"Of course. I'll walk you out," Mama said, standing, but she didn't get far. She stopped dead near the coat closet. "Blue?" She turned to face me. The animals shook again. "What's that smell?"

"It's probably the cat's box," I said, making a beeline for the closet door. I could feel Star's breath on my neck. "I forgot to change it. Sorry."

Beau folded his arms across his white T-shirt. His thumb poked the mermaid's face. "You know, Cecilia"—he started to pace—"I think I smell it, too."

I couldn't stop watching him. He had a regular routine going. *Pace, pace, pace. Stop. Turn.*

The monkey and the seal and the horse clinked hard. Just like they do when a train goes by.

Pace, pace, pace. Stop. Turn.

The lion teetered, closer to the edge.

Mama leaned toward me, sniffing. "It's coming from in there, all right. But it isn't Bud's litter."

Star's breath scorched my neck.

Beau's feet landed harder.

Pace, pace, pace . . .

The monkey and the seal and the horse rattled one final time.

Stop. Turn.

I watched the lion fall. It seemed to move in slow motion. Dropping. Hitting. Bouncing. Snapping apart. Its head landed inches from Beau's left foot. Its body, minus a leg, rolled clear to the kitchen door.

It was like one of those last notes from the music box Pa gave me. Except this time I knew exactly which note was going to be the final one.

Mama glared at me.

The heat on the back of my neck spread through me.

Mama reached behind me for the door handle.

"Blue—" she grabbed the knob. "Move!"

fourteen

Star stepped into the light, squinting like a mole.

"Oh, my God!" Mama's hands flew to her mouth. "Star, I've been so worried about you!"

Star's eyes moved back and forth across Mama's face. Like she was reading and rereading a line she couldn't figure out.

Mama held her arms out, waiting. Just like she'd done with me.

Stewart's horn blew. Two short toots and one long one.

Star hurried past, cat litter crunching on the heels of her boots. "Excuse me," she snapped. "That'll be my ride."

"Your ride?" Mama reached for Star's arm, but she pulled away. "Wait! Why are you leaving?"

Star turned. I could tell she was fighting tears. "I did a lot of thinking this past month, Mama. I wondered if I'd exaggerated everything. Maybe it wasn't so bad there,

I told myself. Or maybe things are different now. Maybe Mama's standing up for herself. Maybe Lyle's straightened himself out. Hell, I even got to thinking about the time he went to bat for me when I got suspended for skipping school."

"You *what?*" Mama started, then stopped herself, looking away.

"The principal called. Lyle talked to him. You were at work. I begged Lyle not to tell you, and he didn't. Three mornings in a row, he picked me up outside school, then dropped me at the library across town so I'd have a place to go. Before I'd leave for the day I'd wet my hair in the bathroom so it'd look like I'd just come from swim practice."

Mama shook her head. "I had no idea."

"I know." Star stepped close to Mama. "Anyway, those are the things I thought about. The nice Lyle. The times he wasn't hurting you. I hated thinking about them because they'd make me question if I'd done the right thing." Her eyes filled as she reached to touch Mama's swollen cheek. "But I'm cured now."

Stewart tooted again.

"Star," Mama began, "I'm sorry for everything."

"Good-bye," Star said, the screen door thudding closed behind her. "I'll miss you."

I waved Mama back and ran after Star, grabbing her arm. My fingers closed around her scar. "Star, please, your leaving isn't going to make it stop."

She pulled away. "Neither is my staying."

Once more Stewart tooted, this time giving us a *What's up?* gesture.

I ran to the cab and stuck my head in the open window. "Here," I said, tossing a twenty-dollar bill on the seat.

Stewart looked confused. "What's this for?"

"Buying time, if that's allowed."

Stewart winked. "Enjoy your talk."

I hurried back to Star.

"Look, Blue—" The veins in her neck stood out. "I've tried."

"I know you have."

"And you've tried."

"I know. . . ."

"Then what's left?" she asked.

"What's left is Mama trying."

"Ha!"

"I'm serious, Star. I think this last fight was different."

"Blue, look at her face. How was it any different?"

"You heard her. She asked for her own room. She tried to get the desk man to protect her."

Star reached inside her backpack for a stick of gum. "What are you saying?"

"Mama never did that before. She always just . . . I don't know . . . *took* it."

"Maybe that's because there was no one around. Just us. And she didn't *have* to ask us to help. We're her kids. Of course we're going to try to do something."

I stared hard at Star. "Except now."

"What?"

"Except now. You're leaving. You're all tried out." Star winced like I'd hit her. I touched her hair, tucking a strand behind her ear. "I understand, though—"

"Don't." She nudged my hand away.

I raised it again, combing my fingers through her short, red strands. Something I remembered Mama doing a long time ago.

Tears inched down Star's pink cheeks.

I made little parts in her scalp with my fingertips.

She moved my hand again, but this time she held on to it. She leaned on a porch rail. I watched it give a little. "I'm tired of the pain. I need a NO VACANCY sign over my heart."

"Tell me about it," I said, leaning beside her. "I'm about to burst. I feel like that dang U-Haul Mama rented after Pa died. Remember that puny thing we tried to cram all our stuff in when Mama had to sell the house?"

"I sure do. *'Gee, girls, think this truck is big enough?'* Remember all the stuff we had to leave behind? What a sin."

"Speaking of sin," I added, "how about Mama—Miss Sunday School Vocabulary—cursing that truck after we'd rearranged it for the hundredth time?"

Now, there was something I'd never forget, the sight of Mama attempting to clutch that fat trash bag filled with Star's and my winter coats and at the same time wedge a box of pots and pans in between Star's stereo speakers and Pa's black velvet painting of the dogs playing poker. I'd never in my life heard Mama swear till then. But she made up for lost time when the handle on her pressure cooker pierced the cigar-smoking pooch through his forehead.

I tugged Star's sleeve. "That reminds me. Remember what Jinx used to say about Mama when they first met? You know, how Mama wouldn't say—"

"Shit," Star whispered, finishing my sentence. I could tell by the way she slumped forward that she was warming up to do her Jinx impersonation. Something, I might add, she did real well.

Star looked to see if Mama was watching. The coast was clear. She dug under her armpit and tipped her butt, letting a phony fart. "Why, Ceil. . . ." Her voice was low and scratchy. She scuffed her feet across the porch, smoking an imaginary cigarette. "Ceil, I swear—you being such a lady and all—why, I bet you wouldn't say *shit* if you had a smelly pocketful."

"That's perfect!" I shouted. I clenched my middle, laughing. "Oh, my God, Star. You are *so* good. . . ."

Star doubled over, too.

I hobbled toward her, still holding my stomach. I got up close and whispered, *"Shit!"*

"Oh, yeah?" Star fell backward against the wobbly railing. It shook something fierce, and she jumped away, her eyes practically bugging out of her head. "Well, *sheeeeee-it* to you, you stupid porch!"

I was gasping for air, sure I'd pee my pants any second.

Star backed against a post, trying to stand. She sucked in her stomach, then blew the words out, hard and fast, in a spray of spit. "Ohhhhhh, shit! Shit! Shit! Shit! Shit! *Shit!"*

"Cripes," I choked out, hooting at the drool on her chin. "Give me a shower, why don't you?"

Star stopped laughing and bolted upright.

I followed her eyes to Mama's solemn face, glaring at us through the screen door.

I don't know what came over me. I looked Mama square in the eye and—before breaking up again—blurted out, "All right, now! Enough of this shit!"

I expected her to come flying out there and give me a royal what-for. Instead she turned back toward the couch, retrieving a tissue she'd dropped.

Star pushed her bangs back. "I should go."

Her skirt dragged the porch steps as she started toward the cab.

I followed her to the end of the driveway.

Stewart leaned out the window. "Star, light, Star, bright. Where we headed to tonight?"

Star didn't answer him. I did. "Back to Springfield." I reached in my pocket, pulled out the wrinkled bills left from Pa's hundred dollars, and stuffed them into Star's hand.

She held out her arms to hug me. "Thanks for understanding. I'll call." She tried to pull away, but I held on.

"When?"

"Soon." She peeled my arms off her neck and set them at my sides like she was posing a mannequin. "You be careful."

I watched her climb in. "You too."

Stewart's radio was playing slow piano music. He put his signal on and waved to me.

I waved back. The truth is, I *did* understand her needing to leave. And if things were different, I could've easily jumped in that cab alongside her, listening to those soft, dreamy notes mush up against each other. 'Cause, after all, there'd been a thousand times in my life—up till then—when I would've walked barefoot to Mars with

Star if she'd asked me to. But this wasn't one of those times.

Stewart tooted. He pulled away.

Star was watching me watch her in the side mirror. She hung her arm out the window and tipped the palm of her hand to face me.

I held mine out, too. I felt a pull, like an invisible string connecting our fingers, stretching thinner and thinner.

The cab edged away. I watched it stop at the red light on the corner.

I could feel the notes of the music inside me. And I could feel the string between Star and me grow stronger as it stretched.

The traffic light turned green. Stewart wasn't moving. A car behind him tooted.

Stewart pulled to the curb.

The door on Star's side flew open.

My heart raced.

Star's boots shot out, followed by the rest of her. Her heels smacked the sidewalk. Her arms flapped at her sides as she made her way toward me. And her lips shaped the same word over and over in between little hiccupy laughs. "Shit . . . shit . . . shit . . . shit . . . shit. . . ."

fifteen

Jinx didn't come home that night.

After supper Star rode her bike to the store for a six-pack of soda while I made popcorn, then the three of us watched *Sunday Night at the Movies,* something we hadn't done together in a long time. Star curled up in her beanbag chair, and I sat beside Mama on the couch. By the time the movie was over, all three of us were fast asleep.

Mama woke first. "Come on," she said, patting our legs, shutting the TV off. "Time for bed."

Speaking of TV, it was like being in a movie, having Star and me walk into our bedroom together for the first time in one whole entire month.

"My bed looks just the same," Star said, kicking her boots off, collapsing backward on her mattress.

"It is. Exactly. Every wrinkle's just how you left it. Mama kept bugging me to make it, but I kept ignoring her."

Star hugged her pillow. "That's so sweet."

By the time I'd changed out of my cut-offs and T-shirt and into my pj's, Star had fallen asleep, completely dressed. A soft snore rattled in her throat. It used to bother me, but not now.

I sat up in bed, savoring the moment. Even though the heat upstairs stuck my back to the headboard, and the smell of garbage rotted in the cans below our open windows, and the awful thought of Jinx coming back played like a sour note through my thoughts—everything, at that moment, was perfect. 'Cause Star was there, her boots parked right beside her bed where they belonged.

Before turning out the light I glanced at a drawing I'd finished recently and thumbtacked to the wall beside my dresser. In it, Pa is leaning over his birthday cake, just about to blow out the candles. His green eyes glitter like emeralds in the flickering light.

I stared hard at his face, feeling something quicken inside me.

A small thing, too new to name.

Come morning, Mama was boiling potatoes for potato salad. She'd made egg salad sandwiches, too, and cut tomatoes into fat red slices, and loaded several colas into a Styrofoam cooler.

"Wow," Star said, sticking her finger in the bowl of leftover egg salad. "Where's the party?"

"I thought we'd have a picnic," Mama said. "At the river."

Star and me exchanged glances.

"Okay," I said. "Why not?"

&

I held the tall brush aside as Mama scooted down the hill of rock, then Star. I went last.

Mama wandered near the tangled, overgrown raspberries.

Star stood at the river's edge. The water was calm. I walked over to her. "You can't step into the same river twice," she said, staring off.

I leaned in close. "Huh?"

"You can't step into the same river twice. A Greek philosopher said it. Things change, in other words."

I looked out at the still blue water.

She was right. It wasn't the same river. In fact, if it could've talked, it would've said something like, *Trust me. I'm not out to hurt anybody.* Why, if the river'd had that same way about it the last time we were there with Pa, he'd still be alive. We'd all be sitting close on the plaid picnic blanket, dangling our feet in the water, eating sandwiches. Star and Pa would go fishing, and there'd *be* no current to sweep him under. There'd *be* no funeral, and there'd *be* no Lyle Thorn. And there'd *be* no bruises on Mama's face.

"Girls," Mama called, "come get something to eat."

Star and Mama sat on opposite corners of the blanket. I flopped down between them. Mama's makeup was pumpkin orange in the sun. She passed us a plate with a sandwich, salad, and a dill pickle. Star tore open the bag of cheese curls, extracting a huge handful.

We started eating, but Mama hesitated. Playing with her napkin, she said, "There's something I need to tell you girls. Something I've been . . . ashamed to say."

Star and me looked up.

"It's about your pa."

"What?" I asked. "What is it?"

"Do you remember the fight your pa and I had that time he took your money?"

Did I! It was a humdinger. Star was off bike-riding with that big-eared Corey boy she had a wild crush on, but I was out back on the swingset. I ducked behind the lilac bushes and heard nearly every word. Pa'd cleared out Star's and my savings accounts—three hundred and eighty dollars in all—and lost every cent at an all-night poker game. Mama was fit to be tied. Pa was apologizing all over the place, stammering up a storm. About the only time he stuttered was when Mama gave him a healthy dose of guilt, and that time his plate was filled to overflowing. I wanted to run inside and yell at her to leave him be. But I didn't. I couldn't figure out which one of them I was more mad at.

Mama popped the top on her soda. "Your pa never touched a dime of your money after that fight. But he laid his hands on mine, all the same. The night after he won the three thousand dollars, after we'd opened our presents and you girls went up to bed"—Mama sipped her cola—"your pa and I had a long talk. Actually, I talked and he listened. I told him the money was to be used to pay back you girls. The rest was to go into the bank, for a rainy day."

I reached for the cheese curls before Star had the whole bag gone. "Mama," Star said, tossing me a look, "that doesn't seem like such an awful thing to say, considering."

"There's more . . . ," Mama said. "Your pa agreed with me. Well, he agreed with the part about paying you girls back, anyway. The second part he didn't go along with. As far as he was concerned, he and I didn't need to save money. If there was enough so I could buy groceries and the electric company didn't shut the lights off, we were set. But I was hoping for more someday. And that money looked like a ticket to whatever that more might be. So I told your pa—"

Star snatched the cheese curls back. "Told him what, Mama?"

"I told him I wanted him to prove to me, once and for all, that his family was more important than gambling. I said the money was to stay put . . . or else."

"Or else what?" I asked.

The sun tucked itself behind a cloud.

Mama hesitated. "Or else I'd leave him."

Star gasped. *"What?"*

"I said I would take you girls back to Tennessee with me, and we'd stay with my family. But I didn't mean it. Not for a second. You girls have to believe me. I was just—well—*bluffing* him, trying to scare some sense into him. Anyway, he got the longest hangdog expression on his face I had ever seen. I knew it'd worked, what I'd said. But, unlike your pa, winning didn't feel that good for me. I knew I'd sucked something vital out of his soul. Still, I convinced myself: It had to be that way. I needed to be the responsible one. I had to make things right. He'd get over it.

"Later that same night, when your pa and I were in bed, I heard him stir. It was close to three A.M. He always got restless then."

"I know," Star said. "That's where I get it from."

Mama flashed a small, sad smile. "I heard him slip his clothes on, then his shoes. I rolled over and touched his arm. 'Roy,' I said, 'please don't go.' He didn't say anything. I listened as he went next door to the bathroom and brushed his teeth and washed his face and gargled. I prayed he wasn't planning to call my bluff.

"I got up shortly after. I hadn't heard the door close or his car start, so I was pretty sure he was still there. He was. Sitting in the living room in the corner chair. It was still dark, of course. I clicked a light on. He was hunched forward, his head in his hands. He was crying. I'd never seen him cry before. I stepped closer. He held his arm out to stop me, but I came to him anyway. I sat on the floor near his feet and laid my head on his knees.

"I hated myself for what I'd done. I'd given that carefree, devil-may-care boy I'd loved so much in high school the heavy heart of a grown-up man. 'I'll change,' he said, choking on his tears. 'I'll do whatever you say.' I squeezed his hand tight. Minutes passed. Hours. Then it was light. I heard you girls getting up, moving around upstairs. Your pa said, 'They can't see me this way.' And he slipped out the front door. At that point, I found myself wishing he *would* take off for Canandaigua. That he'd spend every last cent of that three thousand dollars. He'd see I was still there when he came back, that I didn't mean what I'd said.

"Everything moved so fast after that. You girls came downstairs. I made scrambled eggs and bacon for breakfast. Your pa slipped back inside just as I was setting the table. You both hugged him, same as always. Your pa had a poker face so, as far as you two knew, nothing was wrong. But when I looked across the table at him, I saw the difference.

"Your pa put ketchup on his scrambled eggs that morning. He'd never done that before. And he had two pieces of toast instead of three, and he drank his coffee black. I don't know why I remember these things, but I do. I've been through your pa's last day a thousand times in my head."

Mama turned to Star. "I did the same thing when you ran off. Played everything over and over, raked myself across the coals for every one of my wrongdoings. If only I hadn't yelled at you. If only I'd stayed home that night instead of going out drinking with Lyle. If only I hadn't waited till he went to work to call the police. If only I'd asked to look at your burn." Mama paused, playing with the tines of her plastic fork. "What I'm about to say probably isn't going to make a lot of sense to either one of you, but . . . well, sometimes it's hard to see why it's such a big deal to have somebody beating on you, when you're all the time doing it to yourself already."

Star and me stared in disbelief.

"Mama," I said, "nobody *deserves* that."

"Never mind that for now." Mama reached down, each of her hands seeking one of ours. "Let me finish telling you about your pa. After breakfast, when he stood to put his plate in the sink, he turned and, winking at me, he said, 'How'd the charming Hanson ladies feel about a picnic at the river today?' "

"Wait a minute!" I said. "*I'm* the one who asked Pa to take us to the river!"

"No." Mama shook her head. "That's not the way I remember it."

"It's the way it happened!" I yelled. "I saw how happy everybody was about Pa winning that money the night before. Star had her boots, and you had hope written all over your face. I thought if I came up with something to keep Pa home, to see to it the money stayed put, I could keep things from going bad. That night, before bed, I made Pa promise to take us to the river the next day."

"Whoa!" Star shouted. "Time out! You two can fight all you want about which one of you pressured Pa into going, but you're forgetting something. Going *to* the river didn't kill Pa. Going *in* the river did. If I hadn't begged him to go fishing with me, I would have been the only one looking for that boy when he fell in."

"Your pa would've gone in anyway," Mama said. "That's just the way he was."

"But you and Blue could have held him back. Told him no. And I could've found the boy myself. And Pa, he'd be here." Star fell forward, pounding the empty corner of the blanket with her fists. "Damn it! Damn you, Pa!"

On the next upswing of Star's hands, Mama grabbed them. Star tried wrestling them away, but Mama held tight. Finally, Star toppled into Mama's arms, sobbing. Mama cried along with her, tears burning wide, white trails through her orange makeup.

I slid closer and slipped my arm around Star's shoulder.

The river was smooth, shiny as blue glass.

Pa's ghost was everywhere.

A black bird fluttered close, picked at a speck that floated on the water's surface, then flew off.

"Pa . . . ," I whispered. And I was crying, too.

sixteen

The driveway was still empty. No sign of Jinx.

Mama went in through the kitchen and flipped on the back porch light. The wide yellow triangle fanned out on both sides of Star and me as we sat on the steps, dabbing calamine lotion on our bug bites.

"I've got sixteen of these dang things," I said, counting. "No, wait. Seventeen."

"Numbers are important," Star said. Her teeth were gold in the light. "Some even have special powers. You should always pay attention to them."

I'd missed Star giving me advice on things. I swatted my leg, squashing mosquito guts on my knee. "Eighteen," I said, picking him off. "How's that one grab you?"

Star tipped her head to stare at the half-moon snagged between two trees. "Eighteen is a wonderful number. When you're eighteen, you're an adult. You're free."

"Mama's an adult," I said. "She isn't free."

"Not yet." That is what I *thought* I heard Star say. But it must have been the wind rattling the branches, or my heart, aching so much for certain words it made them up. I asked her, "Did you say something?"

Star stood, then reached her hand down to help me stand, too. "I said, 'Let's go in. It's getting cool.' "

Mama was sitting at the kitchen table, drinking one of Jinx's Miller beers, playing solitaire with Pa's old poker deck.

Star and me started upstairs with a package of cupcakes and a cola. Behind me, I heard Mama mumble something. Star kept climbing, but I walked back to the kitchen. "What, Mama?"

"It wasn't supposed to happen," she said.

At first I thought she meant Pa dying. But then she went on.

"It was our anniversary. We were going to start over. He said things would change. He *promised*." Mama fanned out three cards. She removed the ace and placed it up top, beside the others. "It wasn't supposed to happen. Not there. . . ."

I hugged her from behind, her neck warm on my cheek. "It wasn't supposed to happen *anywhere*, Mama."

She separated three more cards and slapped a red queen on a black king. "I know," she said. "I know."

Star put a record on her turntable and danced toward her dresser, wiping dust off her pyramid rock. "Oh, look!" she said, holding up her bag of M&M's. "I can't believe you didn't eat them!" I beamed with pride as she flopped on her bed and ripped the bag open. Candies flew like confetti across the sheets, collecting in the valleys the wrinkles made.

We finished them off, then Star painted her itty bitty toenails with Shade #23, Chilled Apricot Parfait. When she was done, she announced, "You're next."

"Really?"

She fanned her feet in the air to dry them. "Yes, ma'am. Shade #47, Luminescent Steel Blue. Get it?" She held the bottle out. "For my sister, even if she *doesn't* have her period yet."

I took it from her like I was accepting an Academy Award. "Oh, *thank you, thank you,*" I said, hamming it up.

Star smiled, looping a long snake of cotton between my toes. "I saw one of my spirit guides hovering over us at the river today. A wise old black lady named Esther."

The cotton tickled, but I tried not to move.

Star stroked polish on my big toe. "I think it's so amazing—"

I looked up. "About Esther?"

"No. About how me and you and Mama have been walking around, each convinced we were responsible for Pa's death, not saying a word about it. Not knowing everybody else was feeling the same way."

I stared at my Luminescent Steel Blue toenail, gleaming like a shiny storm cloud. "I'm glad we all fessed up. It felt good to get it out in the open. Kind of like—oh, I don't know—like throwing up."

Star made a face. "Blue, that's disgusting." Ever since the sauerkraut-in-Albany incident, she'd made it clear she'd rather die than vomit.

"No, seriously. . . ." I thought of Stewart's piano music. How it washed through me, making my insides sparkle. That was the feeling I had. Clean. "Except, instead of throwing up food, I threw up *feelings.*"

"Blue, please!"

I didn't try to explain. Star was way too busy trying to stay inside the lines on my crooked baby toe to pay attention anyway.

❦

Mama came up around midnight. We'd left our bedroom door open a crack, and she stuck her head in, whispering good night.

I whispered back.

Star was already snoring. The yellow porch light came in through the window and lit up half her face.

I rolled over on a partly melted M&M, popped it in my mouth, and fell fast asleep.

&

Jinx's truck thundered down the driveway, his radio splitting like an ax through the black night.

Star squinted at the clock's glow-in-the-dark numbers. "It's one-thirty."

I peered out the door as Mama hurried downstairs, wrapping Jinx's robe around her.

Jinx's truck shut off. The night was quiet again, all except for the sound of his boots scraping across the gritty yellow triangle. Uneven scrapes, like he was stumbling.

Mama met him at the back door. Their voices were soft at first. Then Jinx's shot up. "Don't go telling me what time it is, Ceil. I got a watch right here and know full well how to use it, in case you haven't noticed."

Mama said something back.

It got quiet again. Too quiet.

They came upstairs. At first it sounded like they were going to get all lovey-dovey. Their door closed. The bedsprings squawked a few times.

Star and I kneeled on our beds, each pushing an ear against the cool, shiny wall. I'd discovered a while back that if I breathed slow, in and out through my mouth, I could catch prett' near everything.

Must be Jinx brought a beer up with him 'cause I heard a bottle make a *psssst* noise getting opened. Right after, a metal *ping* hit the floor on the opposite side of the room.

Star smiled. "He missed the pail."

Mama's feet padded across the floor. The cap rattled inside the trashbasket. "Lyle," she said, "we need to talk."

"Was that Star's backpack I saw on the couch?" Jinx asked, ignoring her.

"Yes," Mama answered nervously. "I mean, I didn't realize she'd left it downstairs, but, yes, it must be hers. She's . . . Star's back. She came back yesterday. While you were gone."

I listened as Jinx tried to light a match, striking the rough strip again and again, till a spark cracked and a flame hissed.

I looked over at Star's scar. It reminded me of one of those clouds you can see things in. I saw a woman's profile. Maybe it was Esther, appearing from the land of spirits to look after us.

"We gotta set some ground rules for that girl, Ceil. She's getting wild. Running away. Mouthing off. Skipping school—"

"That bastard!" Star whisper-shouted. "He said he'd never tell!"

I thought how easy it is to believe somebody when you really, really need to.

"Next thing you know," Jinx continued, "we're gonna have a juvenile delinquent on our hands."

"Lyle," Mama started. "Star had her reasons for running away."

"Hey, wait!" Jinx said. Paper rattled. "I've got something to show you."

"What's this?"

"It's a house I looked at."

"A house? When?"

"While I was gone, Ceil. I did a lot of thinking—"

"About a house? Lyle, I don't understand."

"I think we should buy it. I'm tired of renting somebody else's stuff. I want something of my own. Look, it ain't much money, not really. We could scrape together a down payment. I got some money in the bank, and, well, didn't you say once you had some socked away from old Roy?"

Star and me glanced toward the music box. *No!* we both mouthed.

The paper rattled again. Mama said, "Lyle, this house is in Otis. Blue and Star would have to switch schools. And it'd be too far for me to drive to work."

"I've been thinking about that, too, Ceil. I think you

should quit your job. It's too much for you, trying to run a house and raise two girls and work besides. I know them damn women's libbers say it's all well and good, but I don't want that for my wife."

"Lyle, I *like* working. And Star and Blue have been through too much to uproot them again."

The glass ashtray on Jinx's dresser clattered as he stamped out his cigarette. I could hear him open another beer. "We got more to consider than those girls, Ceil. What about me and you?"

Mama crossed the room, her feet heavy on the floorboards. "That's another matter."

"Meaning?"

"Meaning we need to talk."

Jinx was just on the other side of the wall, so close I could hear him glug his beer. "Look, Ceil, I know we've got our share of problems. And I want us to work them out. That's why I thought moving to the country'd be good for us. You could keep a garden like you always wanted. Look, Ceil. Just look at this house again. It's even got a damn picket fence. I could just picture some of your fancy flowers growing there. I could never get over the way you knew the names of all of them. I just call 'em 'the red things' or the 'fuzzy purple things,' but you—"

"Aren't you forgetting something?" Mama blurted

out. "You made me a promise, Lyle. Before we went to Cape Cod."

"Ceil," Lyle stammered. "I—"

"Look at my face."

"Ceil—"

"I said *look*."

There was a long silence.

Star threw me a worried glance. I took a slow, deep breath.

Jinx lit another cigarette. Finally, he spoke. "I'm sorry."

Mama's slippers scuffed toward the closet. The door opened. A hanger scraped the rod.

"Did you hear me, Ceil? I said I'm sorry."

"I heard you."

"Well?"

Mama sighed heavily. "Words get used up. Like people. They lose their power."

"And what the hell's that supposed to mean?"

The closet door closed. "I'm tired, Lyle. I'm changing for bed."

"Yeah? Well, I got another take on this. I think it's pretty damn generous of me to even *say* I'm sorry the way you were acting with that bartender. Coming on to him. Asking him for his phone number. But I love you so much I'm willing to forgive you for whatever you did to lead him on. Now, why can't you do the same?"

"Lyle, don't be ridiculous. I liked the plants they had on the windowsills. The bartender wrote down the name of the nursery where they bought them. I thought you and I could stop there on our way back home."

"Sure, sure. And he just *happened* to write it down on his card. Which just *happened* to have his phone number on it."

"That's what he had handy."

Jinx's voice exploded. "No, Ceil, *you're* what he had handy. I saw how he was looking at you."

Star's green eyes filled with fear. They were like Pa's eyes, saying things words couldn't touch.

"Lyle," Mama said, "I told you I was tired."

"Oh, *you're* tired. Excuse me. Well, I'm tired too, Ceil. Tired of this conversation. It ain't exactly going how I'd planned."

Mama's rocking chair made a *whoomp-whoomp* noise. I tried to let the sound calm me. I imagined her sitting there, as she did every night before bed, brushing her hair, smoothing lotion on her hands.

"Who's trying to brainwash you?" Jinx demanded. "Who's trying to turn you against me?"

"Lyle—"

"It's Beau Silver, ain't it? He hasn't stopped pouting since I knocked over his precious table. I guess I need to have a man-to-man talk with him for butting his big nose in where—"

"Beau hasn't said a thing. He drove me back from Cape Cod, that's all."

"Who, then? Star and Blue? You can't let your kids run your life, Ceil. They're biased as hell. No man can ever fill the shoes of the Almighty, Late, Great Roy Hanson. I never stood a chance."

"Lyle, they're scared."

"Scared? Scared of what? Have I ever laid a hand on them?"

"No."

"Damn straight." Jinx crossed the room. "They got pampered lives, Ceil. They want to know scared, they should've grown up with my old man. Now, there's a bastard that'll scare you. 'You don't like them peas and carrots, son?' *Smack!* 'Four Cs and two Ds? What's the matter with you, you dumb shit?' *Slam!* 'What? I broke your wrist? Here, lemme break the other one!'"

"The girls have seen what you've done to me," Mama said. "That's scared them plenty. Unfortunately, it's taken me a while to get it through my head just what they've been feeling but—"

"Oh, boo hoo. Does anybody around here ever think about *my* feelings? Hell, one day I'm a free agent, and the next I got a family of four to support. Nothing's mine anymore. I gotta dig for ten minutes to find a beer in my own damn fridge. I can't even use my own phone 'cause

Miss Congeniality's always talking to her swim buddies or her boyfriends."

"Star's been gone a month, Lyle. I haven't seen you make a single phone call since she left."

"Jesus, Ceil, I'm trying here. I *said* I'm sorry. I *said* I'd buy us a house so we can start over. Star and Blue can have their own bedrooms, like they used to. I don't know what else to do. Can't we forget about yesterday and think about tomorrow?"

Mama was silent. Star reached for my hand, holding tight.

"Ceil? Why aren't you answering me?"

"Lyle, please, let go of my arm. That hurts."

"Well, it hurts me that you're not listening."

"I am listening!"

"No, you're not!"

"Lyle, my arm, you're—ow! *Stop it!*"

Jinx's boots pounded across the floor.

Star squeezed my hand.

"What are you doing?" Mama asked. "Lyle?"

Smash! Plaster crumbled loose inside the wall our ears pressed against.

Star's nails dug in my wrist. "What was that?"

"It sounded like glass," I said back.

Mama attempted to stay calm. "I'm going downstairs for a broom to sweep this up. Let's wait until tomorrow to talk about— Lyle, please, put that down. Lyle, that's the lamp the girls bought me for—"

The whole upstairs shook.

Star and me jumped off our beds, scrambling straight for their room.

The door was locked.

"Let us in!" Star yelled. Her knuckles were bone-white, trying the doorknob, again and again, like turning it the right number of times would make it magically open.

Mama screamed.

I backed up, down the hall. "Out of the way!" I hollered.

"Blue, don't!"

"Move!" My body slammed the door.

Pain splintered through me. Lightning-sharp, zigzagging down my spine.

I fell backward.

Bolted upright.

Tried again. Harder.

I heard Jinx hit Mama. I heard her stumble.

My heart hammered in my throat.

Star pounded the rough wood. "Mama! Mama!" she cried. "Open the door!"

I felt like the Red Rose Tea lion. Close to the edge.

I willed myself not to fall.

"Watch out!" I yelled. I was flying, airborne. *"We're in!"*

And, by God, we were.

seventeen

Mama was holding the spindly desk chair out in front of her.

"No more!" I roared. "NO MORE! NO MORE!" So loud it could've peeled the lilacs off the dingy yellowed wallpaper, could've split the two-by-fours underneath into thick slivers.

I could've roared again. Instead, I saved my strength. I paced the cage, hands knotted.

Jinx grabbed the candlestick on Mama's nightstand, the antique brass one Pa'd bought her. He raised it over his head.

The chair shook in Mama's arms.

He dove at her.

I grabbed the first thing I saw—a large wooden frame holding a picture of Mama and Jinx. I pounced, bringing it down hard on his head.

Glass smashed and scattered. Triangles glistened on the floor.

Jinx wasn't moving.

A cut on the back of his head opened. Then another. Blood wormed out, two dark streams trickling through his thick hair.

I dropped the mangled frame, watching the backs of his legs. Waiting to see if his knees buckled. If his body folded.

It didn't.

Jinx turned to face me, his eyes raging. He crouched forward, arms out, fingers curled like claws. "Look who we got here."

"Blue!" Star yelled. "Get away!"

My muscles clenched and tightened. I stepped forward. Pain pierced my heel. My white sock filled with red.

Jinx wiped sweat off his forehead with the back side of his arm.

We paced in a slow, closing circle.

"Blue, *please!*" Star screamed. "Stop! He'll hurt you!"

I glanced over Jinx's shoulder. Out the window, at clothesline after clothesline stretched like tightropes to the nearest tree. A light came on. Madame Busybody's face flashed across a window, her head full of pink curlers. She was talking on the telephone. Pointing at Jinx and me.

The hair on Jinx's arm brushed mine.

I watched her hang up the phone. I watched for way too long.

Jinx lunged at me. He grabbed my waist, mashing me to his chest, squeezing.

"Put her down!" Mama hollered. I pounded Jinx's back with my fists. My feet flailed at his sides. I tried to knee him in the privates, but his grip was too tight. "Get your filthy hands off me!" I yelled.

Jinx threw his head back, laughing. Phlegm rattled in his throat. "Oh, big tough girl that Blue is—yeah, real tough!" He swung me like we were dancing. "Come on, Blue, show me how tough you *really* are!"

My insides bubbled.

Mama moved closer. "I said put my daughter down!"

Round and round Jinx swung me. If he squeezed any harder, I'd be in two parts.

I screamed. Pounded. Kicked. Screamed again.

Harder and harder he squeezed, swinging me. "Hey, Blue, you're not looking so tough now. *Heh-heh-heh.*"

Round and round and round. Laughing. Squeezing.

Window, wall, bed, door. Window, wall, bed, door . . .

Squeezing. Harder. Spinning. Faster. Thick neck, meaty breath, leather hands, yellow teeth.

Downstairs someone pounded on the door.

Star ran toward the sound.

I couldn't yell. Couldn't roar. I could barely breathe.

Lion on the edge! Lion on the edge!

I saw the brown beer bottle on Jinx's dresser. It flashed by fast. I held my hand out. Grabbed at it. Missed. Tried again.

Footsteps pounded the stairs.

"This way!" Star called. "Hurry!"

Mama lifted the chair over her head.

"Mama," I choked out, "call . . . for . . . help!"

"What?"

"They'll . . . listen . . . this time. *Call!*"

"Help!" Mama cried. "Help!"

"Again!"

"Up here! Help! HELP!"

I reached for the bottle. My fingers closed around its neck.

Jinx laughed. "Tough like your mama, ain't you, Blue? All talk and no show."

I raised my arm over his head. Air flooded my lungs. I roared, baring my sharp lion teeth.

"In here!" Star yelled.

They rushed toward us.

Words blasted from a familiar blond swirl: "Let her go! Now!"

"Now!" a second, darker swirl echoed.

I brought the bottle down hard on Jinx's head. Mama's chair landed next, spindles snapping across his wide shoulders.

Jinx's grip loosened. His arms uncurled. He fell slow and landed hard in a quiet forest of glass shards and spilled beer and broken circles.

The policemen stepped forward.

"We'll take it from here," the one with the blond sideburns said, laying a large, gentle hand on my shoulder.

eighteen

Jinx slumped in the doorway, handcuffed. "Ceil, tell them this is a mistake. Don't let them take me away like this. *Jesus,* Ceil. . . ."

Mama stared at the floor, silent.

I stepped forward, inches from him. The skin on his jaw hung loose. His eyes were dark and watery. "What the hell do *you* want?" he asked.

I didn't need to roar. A whisper's plenty for a broken man. "This is good-bye, Lyle Thorn."

The blond policeman with the bushy sideburns took Jinx to the police station while the shorter, dark-haired one drove Mama and Star and me to the hospital emergency room.

Mama got X rays. I got nine stitches on my left foot

and eleven on my right. And Star got her palm read by a psychic she met while she was waiting for us.

The policeman drove us back to the house.

"Come with me to the cellar," Mama told Star and me.

Star asked, "Why, Mama?"

"Because," Mama answered. "That's where your pa's old traveling bags are. I can't spend another night in this place."

I picked a brown duffel bag that smelled of diesel oil and Dentyne. I crammed it full of clothes and art supplies, then, catching a glimpse of Star's scratchy boots, I wedged Pa's shoeshine tin in there, too. My music box went in last, minus the braid made from Star's and my hair, which I slipped in the side pocket of my jacket. I put Little Ricky in a leftover container and punched some airholes on top.

Mama called Beau Silver, asking him if he'd mind looking after Bud till we found a place that took pets. The Shady Pines Motor Inn, where Mama made a reservation for us, didn't.

Star called Sherry to tell her that Mama was leaving Jinx, so she wouldn't be coming back, but she'd stay in touch.

I made my call last. "We're at that house with the green roof again, Stewart. But this time we're leaving it for good."

Mama shot me a puzzled look. "How do you know this Stewart guy?"

I cupped my hand over the phone. "Just let's get where we're going. I'll give you all the details later."

Star smiled.

Mama shrugged. "Well, okay. . . ."

❧

Our bags were beside the door.

"I think we're ready," Mama said, her hand on the doorknob. "We'll have to come back for the bigger stuff later, once we've got somewhere to put it. Beau'll lend us his station wagon, I'm sure." Her eyes scanned the room like she was half-expecting the furniture to jump up and shout something. She pulled the door closed behind us.

We sat on the porch steps waiting for Stewart. The sun had risen, but the sky was still gray. Scraggly branches raked the house each time the wind blew.

Bud was balanced on my lap in the carrier I'd made— an old brown box from Jinx's cheese factory I'd punched holes in. I pushed two fingers through and he scrubbed his head on my knuckles. I could feel his purr rattling. A rumble like Pa's old rig, only smaller.

"We'll be together again soon," I told him. "You've got my word on it."

Star was chewing Jinx's Beer Nuts in my ear. She leaned in, squinting through a hole. "And if my sister, Blue, gives you her word on something, Old Buddy Boy, you can go straight to the bank with it." It sounded like something Pa would have said.

My eyes dropped to my fat gauzy feet. "Star, *thanks.*"

Star looked up, still chewing. "For what?"

"Oh, nothing."

Stewart's cab pulled close to the curb.

It was starting to drizzle. The tall grass was prickly and damp. I hurried through it, mumbling to any tick who cared to listen, "I *dare* you."

Mama looked over her shoulder before she climbed in. The moist air made her hair hang flat. She brushed it away from her black-and-blue face. "You were right, Blue."

"About what, Mama?"

She slid in next to me. "That house. It couldn't hold a candle to our other one." She was moving something back and forth between her hands. I tried to see what it was, but I couldn't.

Stewart signaled and pulled away. His radio was playing. Slow, moody music that went with the low, thick clouds.

He saw me in the mirror, leaning forward to listen. His eyes caught mine and he smiled. "Mozart," he said. "Clarinet concerto."

I watched the wipers thump and glide on the wet glass. Thump and glide. Thump and glide.

"Mozart," I repeated.

Star checked her watch. The moon symbol had shifted. It wasn't in Aries anymore. I figured—what with that being Jinx's sign and all—it was probably as anxious as we were to get away from anything having to do with him.

Stewart's tires hummed on the bridge pavement. A heavy mist hung close to the water. Mama rolled down her window. Her pale hair blew back, its ends snapping her bruised neck.

Goose bumps inched across my skin.

"Hey, Mama," Star said, shivering. "That's some cold breeze you're letting in."

The river stretched out on both sides of us.

Mama didn't answer her. Drops of drizzle clung to the ends of her eyelashes. She leaned out the window. Leaned far and threw hard, sending that small thing she'd been clutching up, up, into the air, soaring straight for the gray-green water.

I watched it, that little fleck of flying gold, tracking glints of light across the dull sky. Just like a shooting star.

It plinked on the surface of the dark water. Then it sank.

Mama rolled her window up and sat back, rubbing her naked ring finger. Even while the tears came, she smiled.

nineteen

Star and me waited in the cab while Mama carried Bud
up the walk to Beau and Aggie's trailer.

We were parked beside the Dumpsters. A woman in a
yellow rain slicker walked past, a plastic garbage bag in
each hand. A little kid with ashy blond hair like mine
trudged beside her, working hard to keep up as the mud
puddles sucked at her tiny red sneakers.

I was thinking how I'd never be that little again, how
I'd probably get my period any day, when Stewart's arm
stretched across the top of the front seat.

He looked over his shoulder at Star and me. "Your
mama okay?"

I reached in my pocket for the braid. "She will be. We
all will be."

I looked up. I knew he knew.

He turned around farther. "You girls remember now,
you got my number if you and your mama need anything. I mean it."

I fiddled with the hair tie on the braid. "Thanks," I said. "We'll remember."

Mama rushed down the walk toward us, pulling a jacket Aggie'd given her over her head to keep the rain off. She popped the door open and slid in, her damp clothes pressing against my side. "Here," she said, passing around a wet paper bag filled with dark brown muffins. "Aggie made them. Bran."

I sunk my teeth in, remembering the article about fiber I'd read in Mama's magazine. Aggie's muffins were going to see to it none of us got constipated.

We had two each, Stewart included. I licked a finger, dabbing crumbs off my lap. Star had a third.

"Beau and Aggie send their best," Mama said, raising her voice over the hard rain. She eyed my thumb, petting the braid. "Beau said to take a few days off, time to get us settled somewhere."

Stewart backed out past the Dumpsters. I rubbed the mist off my window, looking for the lady with the little girl. They were gone.

My thumb popped through the braid where the hairs crossed.

Mama tugged my wrist. "What's that? Some kind of good luck charm?"

I moved my hand so she could see. "I suppose you could call it that."

Mama laid her fingers across the braid, stroking it like she was stroking the heads it came off. "You think if I cut off a chunk of my hair, *I* could get in on that braid?"

⸙

Star wiggled the key in the door lock. "Seven, two, eight," she said. "Can you believe it? Pa's birthday numbers, July the twenty-eighth!"

Thoughts of Pa swam through me.

Star pushed on the door. "I'd say that's—come on you stupid thing, *open!*—I'd say that's a good omen."

It was as if watching Star open that motel door opened something inside of me, too. I could see Pa. Really see him. Clear as the glass at the Holiday Inn, like he used to say.

"Finally!" she shouted. The door swung open, banging the wall.

I didn't do it, Pa. I didn't make you drown.

Mama pulled a bill from her pocketbook. "Thanks, Stewart."

I figured it out, Pa. The river's got these different faces. And those faces change. Like I've seen ours change—Mama's and Star's and mine—living with Jinx.

Stewart smiled. He had a triangle of bran wedged between his two front teeth.

Pa, the wrong face called to you that day. Just like the wrong face of the wrong man called to Mama after you died.

"You guys take care, now. Tell Blue I said so long. I'd tell her myself but, ah——"

Star elbowed me. "Yeah, I think my sister's in a trance."

Pa nodded like he'd known all along it wasn't my fault. He held his hand out to show me something. The same thing he'd tried to show me in the dream, the thing I'd missed seeing 'cause I woke up. It was something small. Something shiny. I still couldn't make it out.

He was laughing.

What, Pa? What's so funny?

He couldn't stop. He was hooting so hard he was blowing big water bubbles out of his nose, scaring the fish away.

Pa, come on. Tell me!

Pa caught his breath. He reached his hand out. This time I saw it. It was the ring Mama'd thrown in the river. "That cheap good-for-nothing——he——he——" Pa broke up again. "He called this a diamond?"

Pa's laughter flooded through me.

Star shook my arm. "Earth to Blue . . . Blue? Come on, Blue, you're not going to pass out on me again, are you?"

I looked up. It took me a second to focus on Star's eyes. "I'm okay," I told her.

Actually, I was way better than okay.

We put our clothes in the musty dresser. It came out to two drawers each.

I opened the top on Little Ricky's container and put him next to the TV.

Mama sat at the small table in the corner, writing stuff on a note pad she'd found in the desk drawer. The wallpaper vibrated behind her, thick yellow and orange and lime-green lines tipping sideways like Fruit Stripe gum.

Star collapsed on the second double bed. Her skirt fanned out across the orange spread. "Oh, Mama," she said. "I am *sooooo* tired."

"I know," Mama answered. "None of us got much sleep. As soon as I finish this list, I'll shut off the lights and we'll nap some."

Star rolled across the bed, taking the spread with her. She looked like a giant tangerine wedge. "Me and Blue get this bed," she said, chewing a hard candy she'd found in the pocket of Aggie's jacket.

I held my music box on my lap, my fingers resting on its lacquered top.

You're right here with me, Pa. You always will be.

I wound it. The notes pressed in on my stomach.

Pa smiled. The water tugged at him.

Mama ripped her list off the tablet. "After our nap, we'll buy a newspaper and see what's listed for apartments. We'll have to watch what we spend. I know three thousand dollars *sounds* like a lot of money, but by the time I get done paying the first month's rent, then the security deposit . . ."

I turned the word around in my mind. Apartment. *Apartment.* Mama and Star and Blue's apartment.

You hear that, Pa?

I couldn't see him anymore. I could feel him, though. Like I could feel the river inside me. Steady and strong. Always changing but always the same, too.

Star shuffled her tarot cards and arranged them in a cross pattern on the bedspread. The white rectangles quivered against the orange.

"I'm sure this one's meant to be you," she said, tapping the card in the center. I followed her long, peach-colored fingernail to the one she pointed at. "Number eight. Strength."

I sat next to her. "Really?"

She waved her hand over my bandaged feet. "Who else?"

I studied the image on the card. A woman leaned over an animal. A sideways number eight floated above her head. "Hey," I said, "that looks like a *lion* she's petting "

"It is. Why?"

"It's a long story," I said, flopping down beside her.

Star shrugged. Her lips were shiny from the hard candy. She dangled her feet off the bed, pressing, toe to heel, till her boots clunked to the floor. She collected her cards, wedging them back in their pouch.

Mama turned off the light and closed the drapes. She leaned over Star and me, tucking the sheet up under our chins. The room was muggy, but we left it there.

The rain pattered on the roof. The wet streets hissed with tire sounds.

"You two all set?" Mama asked. "You need anything?"

A slice of light from where the drapes didn't close lit up a tear on Star's cheek. "I sure could use a hug if you've got an extra one laying around. . . ."

Mama sat on the edge of the bed. She spread her arms wide, and Star toppled into the open space between them. Back and forth, Mama rocked her. She whispered something in Star's ear. Star's chin puckered, and her bottom lip sucked in and out.

Mama came to my side next. "How about you, Wonder Girl?"

"Well," I said. "You can—if you would, you can—you can wind the music box for me."

Mama crossed the room.

I stared at the indent she'd left on the bedspread.

She walked back, holding the music box, winding it. I could smell the rain in her hair as she leaned close, setting it on the floor beside me. "Anything else?" she asked, waiting.

My words were stuck. I felt clammy. The sheets were glued to me.

There was a long silence.

"It's okay," Mama said, finally. "Maybe some other time—"

"Wait!" I grabbed her hand.

She sat back down. The edge of her face was lit like a crescent moon. "What is it, Blue?"

The notes were slowing down.

"I was wondering if . . ." How could I ask her? I stared at the bruise on her cheek, thinking back on how I'd wanted to shake her myself.

Cripes, isn't there a little bit of Jinx in *all* of us?

Mama's fingers were light as rain, combing my damp straw hair. She took my chin in her hands. "Go ahead. Ask me."

I swallowed hard. "I want . . . I need . . ." I squeezed my eyes shut, but the tears still came. I blurted it out, all at once. "I want you to call me Baby Blue."

My body went limp.

Mama lifted me up from my pillow while I sobbed. "Baby Blue," she whispered, pressing me to her. "Baby Blue, Baby Blue . . ."

The notes in my music box had almost stopped. Mama held me while the last one played. The last note.

I let it go.

"Baby Blue . . . Baby Blue . . . Baby Blue . . ."

I let it go for good.

twenty

The realtor led us up a set of steep wooden stairs. Bread smells from the bakery downstairs drifted through the narrow hallway. She unlocked the door at the top, pushing it open. "Here we are."

An entryway emptied into a small yellow kitchen. A single window lit an old refrigerator, a gas stove, a porcelain sink, and a Formica table with three chairs.

"It's partially furnished," the realtor said.

"That's helpful," Mama answered.

"The landlord lives in Florida. If you decide you'd like to take the apartment, you'd mail the checks there. He allows tenants to make whatever changes they'd like. And pets are okay, as long as they're not loud or destructive."

Mama started toward the bedrooms. There were two. A smaller one with a double bed and dresser and pink walls, and a larger, second one with two twin beds, two dressers, and orange walls. Star took one look at the color and turned to face me, making phony gagging noises.

"Are you all right?" the realtor asked.

Star and me cracked up.

"The living room is this way," she continued, leading us into a room with dark brown paneling, red shag carpet, and a plaid couch. "It isn't Buckingham Palace, but it's reasonably priced."

Mama fished in her pocket for the ad. "How much is it again? We've looked at so many, I—"

"One-fifty a month. And one-fifty security deposit, of course. The rent includes heat and hot water." Her gaze rested on Mama's black eye, which was now a mottled yellow. "And it's available immediately."

Mama pulled the envelope of money from her pocket-book, counting out fifteen twenty-dollar bills. "Here," she said, "we'll take it."

❦

Mama said you can cure many ills with a new coat of paint.

Our first day in the apartment we made a trip to Kmart and chose three gallons: light blue for the hallway and kitchen, peach for Mama's bedroom and the living room, and lavender, the color of Mama's old lilacs, for Star's and my room. Mama placed six eight-by-ten-inch picture frames in our shopping cart as well. "What are those for?" I asked. Most of our photographs were in albums already. And they were smaller than eight-by-ten.

"You'll see," Mama said, strolling toward the checkout.

At eight o'clock that night, we finished painting the living room. Mama had a large pepperoni pizza delivered. We plopped down on the drop cloth, spattered from head to toe with peach paint, admiring our work.

"I think the place has potential," Mama said, picking the pepperoni off her slice, laying it on a napkin beside her.

This time Star didn't gag. We both nodded in agreement.

The next morning I woke to a surprise.

Mama had collected several of the drawings I'd thumb-tacked over my dresser and placed one in each of the six frames she'd bought the day before. They lined one wall of our freshly painted living room. Mama sat on the couch, sipping coffee, smiling up at them as Pa's old transistor radio played softly on the end table beside her.

"So," she asked, "what do you think?"

"Wow," I said, blushing, walking from one to the next. I felt like I had my very own art gallery.

I paused in front of the portrait of Mama and Star I'd sketched from an old photo Pa took one Christmas. Mama was holding up a set of plug-in rollers she'd just unwrapped while Star hugged her Magic 8 Ball. I sat off to the side, Spirograph wheels spilled around me like snow. Half of me was cut off; one ear, one elbow, and one foot made it into the picture.

"Your pa couldn't center a photograph to save his soul," Mama said, reading my thoughts.

I smiled back. And not just 'cause of what Mama'd said about Pa. I had an idea. And, someday—soon, I hoped— I'd turn that idea into something.

᠁

I had my thirteenth birthday in our new apartment. Star got me a beautiful amber-colored glass lion and a large heart-shaped candle. We had dinner at Shorty's Barbecue, just like we used to, then walked to the art store, where Mama let me pick out my present. I chose a small table easel; a package of canvas boards; and a starter set of oil paints that contained eight colors, a tiny jar of turpentine, and three different-sized brushes, all with bristles the color of Star's hair.

I set the easel in the corner of our bedroom and began a painting the very next day. I didn't look at a photograph this time. Instead, I sat with my face centered in the small pedestal mirror Mama'd let me borrow from her dresser. I squeezed burnt sienna onto my palette, thinning it with turpentine. Brush in hand, I sketched in the outline of my face, then the guidelines—where my eyes would go, my nose, my mouth—just like my art teacher, Mrs. Mosher, had shown us in class.

In the bathroom next door, I could hear the *tsssssst* of Mama's hair spray. She was leaving soon to register for two night classes at the community college: Operating a Small Business and Flower Arranging. One night during supper she'd started talking about her flower shop dreams again. Instantly I recalled how the four of us—Mama and Pa and Star and me—would sit around the kitchen table in much the same way, playfully arguing over what Mama should call her shop. Star insisted on Floral Ambience. I liked Bouquets and Such. And Pa stood by Cecilia's Camellias. Mama never let on which one she favored.

The phone rang in the kitchen. I held my breath like I always did. Lyle'd gotten our phone number from the operator, and he called every day from jail, begging Mama to take him back when his sentence was up.

"It's for me!" Star hollered. "It's Charlie!" I let my breath go. Charlie was a boy Star'd met at the bakery downstairs. They were going to see a movie at the cinema downtown.

Moments later, she burst into our room, slipped a 45

on her turntable, and began changing her clothes for the ten zillionth time. A blue gauze shirt flew toward the mound of cast-offs gathered at the bottom of her bed. Bud, who'd settled on my pillow, lifted his head, watching her.

Once changed, she turned to face me. "How does this look?"

"Great."

"Are you sure?"

"Positive."

"Is this outfit better than the other one?"

"Which one?"

"All of them."

"Definitely."

"Thanks." Star flashed me a wide smile and bounded down the hall.

Her record ended. The arm shimmied back and forth in the last groove. I swizzled my brush in the turpentine and reached for the album I'd bought with the ten dollars Beau and Aggie had given me for my birthday. I laid the arm in the groove. A Mozart clarinet concerto swelled the walls of our lavender room.

Mama appeared at the bedroom door. "I'm leaving, Blue. Make sure you lock up behind me. And if Lyle calls—"

"Mama, don't worry, I'm not going to give out our address."

"I know." She started toward me, then stopped. "That smell . . . ," she said. And I knew she was thinking the same thing I did when I first uncapped that small jar of turpentine: *It's a Pa smell.*

I inhaled deeply, too.

Pa leaned on the hood of a car I had never seen before. Grease smudges lined his forehead and dust danced in the beam of light the skinny window let in. I studied the page on the calendar over his worktable. An open footbridge stretched between two hills. One was Pa's hill, far off but still reachable. The other was mine. Right here. Right now. I didn't ask what it was called this time. It was our bridge, Pa's and mine, and I would be the one to name it.

I blinked. My face flashed in the mirror. For a moment I didn't recognize myself. Maybe I'd caught a glimpse of that person Mama'd told me I'd one day see.

Mama stepped forward, kissing the top of my head. Our eyes met in the glass. "Sure you don't mind being alone for a while?"

"No," I answered her reflection. "I'm going to work on my painting. I'll be fine."

She crossed the room, pausing at the door. "Oh, Blue . . ."

"Yeah?"

"If I ever do have my own flower shop, I like Bouquets and Such the best. But do me a favor. Don't tell your sister."

"Deal."

I could tell she was nervous by the way she kept smoothing her skirt. "Well, I guess this is it," she said, turning. "Cecilia Hanson Thorn is off to make something of herself."

So am I, I thought.

And as I painted in the almond-shaped outlines of my eyes, I knew I had already started.

author's note

In 1976, when *Baby Blue* is set, there were no laws in place in the state of Massachusetts to protect victims of domestic violence. Assault and battery, if not witnessed by a police officer, was considered a past misdemeanor, and an arrest could not be made. The most police were empowered by law to do was to remove the assailant for a reasonable period of time for "cooling off," after which he would be returned home and, most likely, batter again.

In 1978, the Abuse Prevention Act (Chapter 209A) was passed, creating the first protective order available to battered parties and their children in the state of Massachusetts. (By 1980, forty-six other states had similar laws.) The Abuse Prevention Act was amended in 1983 and again in 1987. By 1990, a law enforcement officer could make an arrest based on probable cause, meaning it was not necessary for police to witness an assault, only to have reason to believe an act of abuse had occurred. Today, all police officers in the state of Massachusetts undergo 209A training and work closely with shelters, counselors, and district courts to assist victims. Emergency protective restraining orders can be issued anytime, day or night, at no cost.

The National Domestic Violence Hotline provides crisis intervention and referrals to emergency shelters and services across the country twenty-four hours a day. Their toll-free number is 1–800–799–SAFE.

DATE DUE
